GRANDMOTHER • GOES
UP • THE • MOUNTAIN

Margaret Kitchen

GRANDMOTHER · GOES
UP · THE · MOUNTAIN
and
Other Mexican Stories

◆

Illustrated by David Pike

ANDRE DEUTSCH

First published in 1985 by
André Deutsch Limited
105 Great Russell Street London WC1B 3LJ

Text Copyright © 1985 by Margaret Kitchen
Illustrations © 1985 by David Pike
All rights reserved

Phototypeset by Falcon Graphic Art Ltd
Wallington, Surrey
Printed in Great Britain by
Ebenezer Baylis & Son Ltd, Worcester

British Library Cataloguing in Publication Data

Kitchen, Margaret
    Grandmother goes up the mountain
    and other Mexican stories.
    I. Title   II. Pike, David
823'.914[J]   PZ7
ISBN 0–233–97749–X

CONTENTS

Grandmother Goes Up The Mountain   1

The Carnival Thief   38

Ghosts in the Convent   63

Tepingo Treasure   106

GRANDMOTHER · GOES
UP · THE · MOUNTAIN

Pepita woke up before the first light of day. She was lying in bed beside two of her four sisters. She looked up through the straw roof of their small wooden house and saw the last stars of the night still shining in the sky.

She didn't usually wake up so early and she wondered why she was awake so early today.

There must be a special reason because she felt very excited. But it wasn't her birthday, or her saint's day, so why did she feel butterflies in her tummy?

She tried to remember whether anyone else in her large family had a birthday today, but she couldn't think of anyone.

So what was it?

Why was she so sure today was a special day?

She rubbed her eyes and tried to remember.

'Oh yes,' she said suddenly out loud so her little sisters stirred in their sleep. 'Of course! I know why today is special. It's the day of the ancestors.'

Pepita had only learned what the word 'ancestors' means the day before. Her grandmother had told her that ancestors were people who were members of the family a long time before Pepita and her family were born.

Even a long time before grandmother was born and that seemed a very long time ago.

Although the ancestors had lived a long time ago in the village of Tepingo where Pepita and her family lived, the villagers still liked to remember those people who had lived so long ago.

So, every six years they held a festival to remember the ancestors. It was a very grand festival. People came from all the villages around the valley, and some people even came from the big city, to see the splendid ceremony which was held at the top of the mountain.

It was held at the top of the mountain because the ancestors had built a pyramid there and during the ceremony the villagers would sing the songs and dance the dances which the ancestors sang and danced in their own ceremonies.

'Well, if I'm eight,' thought Pepita, 'that means I was two the last time they had the festival. I don't remember that one, but I will remember this one. It's going to be a very good one.'

Someone was moving about in the room. There were only two rooms in the small wooden house in the corner of a field. Ten people lived in those two rooms: Pepita, her four sisters, two brothers, her mother, her father and her grandmother.

It was her grandmother who was moving in the room now, and Pepita heard her calling softly: 'Pepita, Pepita you must get up.' Grandmother knew that Pepita was always the first sister to wake up, particularly on special occasions.

'But Little Grandmother, I do not have to go to school today,' complained Pepita, pulling the blanket up to her ears.

'I know, I know, but there is much work to be done. Today is the day of the festival of the ancestors. You must go to the village and grind the corn so that I can make the tortillas early today.' Grandmother's voice was very firm.

'Oh, grandmother, why must it always be me?'

'Because you work hard, Pepita, your brothers are lazy and your sisters are too young. Hurry now, it will soon be light and then there will be too many people waiting to grind corn.'

Pepita jumped out of bed and pulled on her dress. She quickly made her long dark hair into a pigtail and pushed her feet into her sandals. She picked up the basket of corn and walked outside.

It was getting light now and the chickens and pigs were beginning to make noises. As she walked through the yard she saw the turkeys climb into their usual tree.

Every morning at six o'clock they climbed into that tree and gobbled away at each other. They did the same thing every evening at six o'clock too. In Tepingo the animals were the village clock. The one on the wall of the town hall had stopped years ago, and nobody had bothered to repair it.

Out on the road Pepita met her friend Maria who was also carrying a basket of corn to grind in the market place at the tortilla stand.

'We're up early this morning,' Pepita called as she waited for Maria to catch up with her.

Maria didn't like work very much, but there was always such a lot of work to do in a big family.

The boys worked on the land with their fathers and the girls worked in the house helping their mothers to make the food and wash the clothes. Pepita didn't think it was fair that only the boys could work in the fields, and that they never had to wash clothes. But that was the way of the village and things didn't change much in Tepingo.

'It is exciting isn't it?' Pepita said to Maria. 'Imagine. We are really going to climb the mountain in the procession and see the dancing and the chanting.'

'What's chanting?' asked Maria.

4

'Grandmother told me that it's a kind of singing of the old stories of the village, which the elders will chant in the language of Nahautl.'

'Why in Nahautl? We won't understand a word,' complained Maria frowning.

'Because that was the language of the ancestors and many of the elders in the village understand it. Grandmother does, and she says it is a pity that we don't.' Pepita skipped merrily ahead of Maria.

'I can't wait to see everyone dressed in the beautiful costumes like the ancestors wore and watch everyone dance around the pyramid,' she called out over her shoulder.

'First we have to climb up to the pyramid. Right to the top of the mountain and that's going to take a very long time,' said Maria a little gloomily.

'Yes,' said Pepita, 'We have to start at two o'clock and everyone will take their food and there will be a big party. It will go on all night.'

'Will we sleep up there?'

'Yes I suppose we will.'

'Won't it be scary?'

Pepita laughed. Maria was always scared of something. Pepita wasn't very often scared of anything.

'Not with so many people there, Maria,' she replied. 'All the village is going, everyone will be there. Grandmother says the spirits of the ancestors live there and they will be happy that everyone is going to visit them, but you can't see them, they're just there.'

5

The two girls looked at each other. They were already happily thinking about what was going to happen and a little bit nervous as well, after all, this was their first festival of the ancestors.

When they arrived at the market square there were already a lot of people there. Some of the people who sold things had been sleeping on the ground all night. They came from villages a long way away and they walked to Tepingo to sell their fruits and vegetables in the market early in the morning before the sun got too hot.

It was going to be a very big market that day, because all the families were preparing special meals to take to the top of the mountain, and all the families in Tepingo were very big families.

The market place looked really lovely with piles and piles of brightly coloured fruits and vegetables all set out on the ground under canopies.

The two girls went to the tortilla shop in the corner of the square and paid five centavos to grind the corn that they had brought with them.

Dona Leonora had owned the grinding machine for a long time, she was the only person in the village who had one. It was very old, but it made the corn into a paste called maza and from this the women of the village made tortillas, which are round and flat like pancakes.

The people of Tepingo eat tortillas with all their meals. They roll them up and eat them in their hands with a plate of beans. Sometimes, when the family has some meat they chop it up and fill the tortilla with it. Then they put hot chilli sauces over the meat and roll up the tortilla. This is called a taco.

'So, girls,' said Dona Leonora. 'You will climb the mountain today, no?'

'Yes,' said Pepita and Maria nodding their heads.

'Do you have your costumes ready?'

'Oh yes,' they said.

The women of the village had been sewing the costumes for many months. Even the poorest families would be dressed in a special way. The older people would wear masks on their faces and the young women would have flowers in their hair.

The women wore simple white dresses with lots of embroidery around the neck, the sleeves and the hem.

'Your mother has been busy I expect?' Dona Leonora said to Pepita.

Pepita's mother was famous in the village for her wonderful embroidery.

Pepita blushed, she was very proud of her mother.

'Yes, she has, we have beautiful dresses for today.'

'And what has she embroidered on your father's cape this year?'

All the men in the village wore short capes around their shoulders for the day of the ancestors, with something special embroidered on the back.

'A jaguar,' answered Pepita.

'Ah yes, the jaguar,' said Dona Leonora. 'On the pyramid at the top of the mountain there are many faces of jaguars.'

'Why?' asked Maria, who never remembered what she was taught in school.

'Because,' replied Pepita, filling her basket with maza and

8

putting a cloth on the top to keep the dust off, 'the ancestors carved them into the rock of the pyramid.'

'There used to be a lot of jaguars around Tepingo,' said Dona Leonora, 'and the ancestors used them as a symbol on the pyramid. This would have been the year of the jaguar for the ancestors.'

'There aren't any real ones now are there?' asked Maria, looking scared again.

'No,' laughed Dona Leonora, 'don't worry, Maria, you will be quite safe.'

The two girls set off along the road back to their homes. As they walked they looked up at the mountains in front of them.

They weren't *really* mountains, but very, very tall rocks which everybody always called mountains.

'Can you see the pyramid?' Pepita asked Maria.

'Stop! let's look for it,' cried Maria standing on one foot in the middle of the road as she concentrated on the view in front of her.

In the early morning light, with a mist still floating over the mountains, it wasn't easy to spot the pyramid. There were so many rocks of so many different shapes and they were looking for a pale square shape almost at the top.

'There it is, there it is, I see it,' Maria said, jumping up and down. 'Look, follow my finger.'

Sure enough, Pepita could see it too, at the end of Maria's finger, very, very, high up.

'Goodness, we do have to go a long way, don't we?' she said.

'Yes we do,' answered Maria and then she looked puzzled. 'How are we going to get our grandmothers up there?'

Pepita hadn't thought about that at all.

'I don't know,' she said, 'I don't know, Maria.'

And as the two girls said goodbye Pepita walked home thinking about it.

———

The whole family was in the yard when Pepita arrived home. Mother was already washing clothes, the boys were feeding the animals. Father was chopping wood for the stove and her sisters were washing their hair in a tub and splashing a great deal of water about in the process.

'Pepita, Pepita,' the little girls came running up to her all talking at once.

'Imagine, today we don't have to go to school.'

'It's a festival. You are going to climb the mountain with Pancho and Antonio and Mama and Papa, but we can't go.'

'They say we are too young.'

'It isn't fair.'

'But we are going to stay here with Grandmother and our cousins and eat special cakes and dance.'

'Are you excited, Pepita?'

The noise from the four little girls was tremendous and Pepita tried to quieten them down.

'Yes, yes I am excited,' she said. 'Don't worry, you will go when you are all bigger. I didn't go the last time, either. But what do you mean you are going to stay with Grandmother? Isn't she going too?'

Just then Grandmother called Pepita from behind the house.

10

She was sitting under a small straw roof waving a fan in front of the comal, a small fire covered with a piece of iron, where she was going to make the tortillas. Pepita went to her.

'Here is the maza, Little Grandmother. I think we will have to make many tortillas today.'

'Yes we will, sit down and help me.'

Pepita sat with her legs crossed on the floor. It isn't easy to make tortillas, but Pepita had learned from Grandmother since she was very young.

She took a small piece of the maza in her hands and rolled it until it was soft and then patted it very fast. Like magic it soon became a small circle and then a larger circle, until it was the size of a small plate. Then she put it on the comal to cook and started to make another one.

They worked very fast. The family had to eat tortillas with their beans for breakfast and they needed many more to eat at the big feast of the day.

'Grandmother,' began Pepita as they worked. 'Why aren't you coming up the mountain with us?'

Grandmother smiled.

'I'm too old, Pepita, too old. I've been many times before, I will stay and take care of the little ones.'

'Did you go the last time? Six years ago?'

'No, I stayed to take care of you and your brothers. The old don't climb mountains, even mountains which aren't really mountains. I have had my time, now is the time of the young.'

'Grandmother, did you always climb with Grandfather up the mountain?'

11

'Yes, of course I did. We climbed the path together even when we were your age.'

'Wouldn't you like to go one more time, Grandmother?'

'Now, Pepita!' Grandmother said sternly. 'Enough of this nonsense. We must finish the tortillas.'

The old lady bent her head over the comal and turned the tortillas.

But Pepita was thinking. She had an idea. Pepita could never sit still when she had an idea. She got up and went to look for her brothers.

'Hey, there,' she called when she found them in a field. As usual Pancho and Antonio were boxing.

They hadn't stopped boxing since they had been to see a boxing match on Dona Leonora's television. Boxing was the most important thing in the world to them at the moment.

'Hey, you two, come here,' she shouted even louder, almost stepping on a small piglet as she did so.

'What do you want,' Pancho shouted back without stopping. The boys did not like having their boxing matches interrupted.

Pepita thought they were rather silly to spend so much time beating each other up, but on the other hand there were times when she could have done with a good boxing match herself.

'Oh do stop fighting and come here you couple of idiots,' she yelled impatiently. 'I want to talk to you about Grandmother.'

The boys stopped boxing instantly. Grandmother was important. They came running up to Pepita.

'What's the matter with Grandmother?' they asked anxiously.

'Grandmother,' said Pepita looking very seriously at the boys, 'wants to go up the mountain today with us.'

'How do you know?' they asked.

'I just know,' replied Pepita.

'Well why doesn't she come then?' asked Antonio innocently.

'Because she's old, obviously,' Pepita glared at her younger brother. 'But we have got to think of a way of getting her up the mountain.'

Pancho looked pensive. He had been up the mountain before with his father and he knew what a steep and rocky path it was. He just couldn't imagine how Grandmother would make it up there.

'But, Pepita,' he said, 'the path is very rocky and difficult, we shall have to be very careful ourselves and it takes many hours to climb. Grandmother is too old to go.'

'But she must go again, as she did with Grandfather since they were children, it means so much to her.' Pepita knew it was very important to Grandmother even though Grandmother would never admit it.

'You are right,' said Pancho, kicking the ground. 'But how on earth are we going to do it?'

The three children stood staring at the mountains surrounding the village thinking and thinking of a solution. Then Mother's voice called out to them.

'Come along you three. What are you doing? Come and eat breakfast, there is much work to be done.'

The donkeys were stamping their feet in the yard as the family sat down around the comal to eat their beans and tortillas.

Every morning the two donkeys took the boys and their father to the fields where they worked. Every morning except Sunday.

13

Today was Thursday. They were ready to go and nobody was going to take them, they didn't understand it was a holiday.

Antonio had an idea.

'Maybe,' he whispered to Pepita and Pancho, 'We could take Grandmother up the mountain on a donkey?'

Pancho shook his head.

'The donkeys are too old, they can hardly walk to the fields any more. The path up the mountains is much too steep and rocky for them.'

Just then the village brass band marched through the gate into the yard playing music very loudly.

Everyone jumped up in excitement and Grandmother went off to find more of the small brown bowls to fill with beans for the players.

The band made a lot of noise and Rosita, the littlest sister of all, ran to her mother covering her ears with her hands.

'Why have they come,' she asked and her mother laughed.

'They always come when there's a festival. They visit every house in the village.'

The yard was in uproar. The music played loudly and the pigs squealed. The chickens screeched, the turkeys gobbled and the donkeys stomped. The children started dancing and their father brought out his drum and drummed in tune to the music. Everyone was very happy and even Rosita forgot she was frightened and began to dance too.

It was only half past seven in the morning but the festival had already begun for the Jiminez family.

When everybody was tired they all sat down on the ground and Grandmother served them beans.

14

'The musicians must get very fat if they eat beans at all the houses in the village,' said Rosita as she watched the men eat hungrily.

Everyone laughed.

'Mmm,' said Pepita, 'but they must be very strong.' She looked very hard at Pancho who instantly knew what she was thinking.

'No, Pepita,' he hissed. 'They can't carry Grandmother. They have to carry their instruments to play at the top of the mountain.'

Pepita shrugged her shoulders and sighed.

'Anyway,' added Pancho 'I don't think Grandmother would let anyone carry her up the mountain.'

Pepita was beginning to think her two brothers were not going to be much help in getting Grandmother up the mountain.

The band went away to the next house and the family went back to work. The two boys went to the village square with their small wooden boxes to clean shoes and Pepita went to the river with Grandmother to wash dishes.

'Grandmother, you are going to come up the mountain with us today. I know you are, I don't know how you are, but I'm sure you are.'

Grandmother laughed. 'Pepita, you are such a dreamer.'

'No, Grandmother.' Pepita looked very serious. 'You know you want to go, and you must believe you will go. That will help me to find a way.'

Grandmother looked at Pepita's serious face.

'Very well, I'll believe,' she said and she picked up the dishes and walked slowly away from the river.

The day was starting to get hot. It was always very hot in the village of Tepingo, which is why people tried to get as much work done as possible in the early morning.

Pepita was worried. Time was going by quickly and she still hadn't thought of a way of getting Grandmother up the mountain.

She sat by the river thinking and thinking. In the village she could hear the noise of the band playing and the people dancing. Soon the cooking would begin and she would have to help mother prepare the food. At two o'clock the long walk up the mountain would begin.

'What can I do?' Pepita said to a lizard who was staring at her from a stone on the other side of the river. But the lizard just stared back.

'Why can't I fly like you so I could carry Grandmother on my wings?' she asked a passing butterfly. But the butterfly just fluttered on. 'Why aren't I big and strong so that I could carry her on my back?'

Suddenly there was a loud moo from behind her and Pepita jumped.

Don Pedro's cow Esperanza had escaped from the field. Again. Esperanza was always escaping; she didn't like being shut up in a field. She liked to be free. So did Pepita, so she and Esperanza often went for walks together and Pepita told Esperanza about all her plans for the future.

Pepita had many plans. One day she would leave Tepingo and go to the big city. But first she had to grow up and that seemed to be taking a very long time.

Esperanza always listened to Pepita very sympathetically. She would like to see the city too but she didn't think Don Pedro would ever take her there and it was a very long way away for a cow to walk by herself.

'Hello, Esperanza,' said Pepita. Esperanza looked at Pepita with her big brown eyes.

'No, we can't go for a walk today, Esperanza, there's too much work to do. It's the festival of the ancestors. I wonder whether cows have ancestors?'

Esperanza looked blank.

'Come on, I'm taking you home,' and the two walked off along the river until they came to Don Pedro's house.

He was outside polishing his shoes. Pepita had never known Don Pedro to polish his shoes before. In fact he didn't very often wear shoes.

'Are you going to climb the mountain in those shoes, Don Pedro?' she asked.

'Yes I am, little one,' he replied.

'But they will get dirty.'

'Yes, but I can't possibly wear my festival costume without cleaning my shoes.'

'No, I suppose not,' Pepita said a little doubtfully, 'I brought Esperanza back. You don't want to lose her today there's so much to do.'

'No I don't. Thank you, Pepita. Why are you looking so worried?'

'I have a problem,' Pepita said scratching the ground with a stick.

Don Pedro looked serious. Pepita remembered that Don

Pedro was very good at solving problems, so she decided to tell him about hers.

'It's Grandmother, you see,' she began. 'Grandmother has to go up the mountain with us, I know she really wants to. But how are we going to get her up there?'

'Why does she have to go, Pepita? She's very old, you know,' asked Don Pedro.

'That's exactly why she has to go – just once more. Like she did with Grandfather since they were very young.'

Don Pedro had been Grandfather's best friend.

'Yes, I see your problem,' he said. And he closed his eyes and started to think.

Pepita sat on the ground and watched his face while he was thinking. A lizard crawled by and a humming bird was humming in the tree beside the house. Lots of noise was coming from the village as everybody prepared for the festival.

The dogs were barking around the square because they didn't like the noise of the band. And up in the hills outside the village somebody was letting off firecrackers. It was never quiet in Tepingo. Not even for a minute. Not even at night.

Suddenly Esperanza gave a loud moo and Don Pedro opened his eyes.

'Of course,' he said, slapping his thigh. 'Esperanza will take Grandmother up the mountain!'.

Pepita looked at him to see if he was really serious.

'Esperanza?' she asked amazed.

'Yes, of course,' he laughed. 'Esperanza has been up the mountains many times before.'

18

'But the path is very rocky and difficult for people with two feet, how can a cow with four feet manage?'

'Oh, Esperanza has very steady feet and she loves to climb mountains. Anyway four feet are better than two for climbing, Esperanza should have been a mountain goat really. I have a special seat which we'll put on her back and your grandmother will be very comfortable.'

Pepita jumped up and danced around Esperanza happily.

'I'm so glad, I'm so glad. Esperanza and Grandmother will both go up the mountain, I'm so happy.' But suddenly she stopped.

'How,' she said very seriously indeed, 'will we ever convince Grandmother to ride on a cow?'

Don Pedro hadn't thought of this. He closed his eyes again and Pepita sat on the ground.

'Well, Pepita,' he said after a while, 'I remember during the war of the revolution when the people had to live in the hills to hide from the soldiers, a lot of the old people rode up on cows as well as donkeys and everyone was very proud of them. We will tell her that we will be very proud of her if she rides on Esperanza but first we must tell your family so that they will help us to convince her.'

'Oh yes, they will be very proud of her,' said Pepita. She thought Don Pedro was very clever, but she also thought he too must be very old if he could remember the revolution so well.

She looked worried again. And then she realised.

'But Don Pedro, Don Pedro, I think you were going to ride on Esperanza, weren't you? Oh yes, you were, you were.'

Don Pedro's face had turned very red. He looked a little sad and didn't say anything for a moment.

'Well yes, yes I was going to, Pepita. But I went to the festival last time and your grandmother didn't. You are right she always went to the festival with your grandfather and I went with them because we grew up together. I think she should go this time with you.

'I will take my flute and play to the little children who are left behind. I'll play so well you'll hear me at the top of the mountain. Your grandfather was my best friend and I know he would be very happy if your grandmother went up the mountain today.'

'You are very kind, Don Pedro.'

'No, little one, it is an honour to do this for Dona Marcela. Now come along and we will go and talk to your family.'

Don Pedro took his hat from the nail on the wall of the house and began to walk out on to the road. Esperanza followed him and Pepita skipped along behind them looking happily up at the pyramid on top of the mountain.

———

'Go up the mountain on a cow!' Grandmother's voice boomed around the yard. She was still sitting in front of the comal making more and more tortillas.

'What a lot of nonsense you do talk, Don Pedro, now leave me alone, I have a lot of work to do.'

'Grandmother, listen to him please,' said Pepita desperately.

'Yes Mama, *do* listen,' said Pepita's mother who was as excited as Pepita about the idea.

20

'You too?' said Grandmother looking severely at her daughter. 'You're all quite mad. I am an old woman, my place is here beside my comal taking care of my grandchildren, not climbing mountains. Least of all on the backs of cows.'

By now the whole family had come into the yard to find out what was going on. Even the turkeys were strolling around the comal bobbing their heads up and down as though they were considering the problem. Grandmother shooed them away impatiently.

Esperanza stood serenely in the middle of the group of humans, watching them lazily, flicking her tail to brush off the flies. The sun was climbing higher, the day was getting hotter and nobody could persuade Grandmother to say yes.

Really. If somebody didn't do something soon Esperanza was going back to the river. She needed to rest if nobody else did, it was a long way up that mountain.

'Grandmother, Little Grandmother, do please say yes, we all want you to go up the mountain with us, please say you will.' Pepita was almost in tears.

'If I go up that mountain, which I won't, I will go up on my own two feet, not on the back of that crazy cow.'

That did it! Esperanza took offence at being called crazy. Everybody always thought she was crazy. She tossed her head and trotted out of the group and headed off in the direction of the river.

'*Now* look what you've done, Dona Marcela,' said Don Pedro to Grandmother. 'You've upset Esperanza.'

Grandmother shrugged her shoulders and threw another tortilla on to the comal.

21

'Dona Marcela,' Don Pedro's voice was very firm, ' do you remember the year of the serpent when Dona Carola wanted to go to the pyramid for the festival? She had been ill for a very long time. Everyone knew she couldn't make it to the top.'

'I remember, I remember,' said Grandmother slowly patting a tortilla between her hands, looking at the comal.

'And in the end she went up the mountain. Not on a cow or a donkey. But how? On the shoulders of young Pepe Gonzalez, that's how! True or not Dona Marcela?'

'True, true,' said Grandmother, 'he was very strong.'

'So is Esperanza, Grandmother, and much more comfortable than Pepe's shoulders,' said Pepita hopping from one foot to another in great agitation.

'And who . . .' began Don Pedro, pausing to look sternly at Grandmother who avoided his eyes, 'who persuaded Dona Carola to go up the mountain on Pepe's shoulders?'

Grandmother bent her head over the comal and didn't answer. There was silence in the group standing around her. Even the turkeys stopped gobbling. Pepita held her breath. Nobody moved.

All of a sudden Felipe, Grandmother's blue parrot, fluttered down from the tree above the comal. Nobody had noticed him perched up there, but Felipe was usually around when Grandmother needed him. He landed on Grandmother's shoulder.

'Marcela,' he squawked loudly in her ear. 'Marcela.'

The beginnings of a smile appeared at the corners of Grandmother's mouth. Don Pedro gave a snort, and Pepita's father sat on his heels rocking backwards and forwards in silent laughter.

And then everybody in the yard in front of the little wooden house began to laugh and laugh. The children, the grown ups and even the turkeys it seemed, laughed and laughed. They laughed so much everyone had to sit down on the ground, except Don Pedro, who stood there wiping his brow still waiting for Grandmother's reply.

'Well?' he almost shouted, 'Who persuaded her?'

'I did,' Grandmother shouted back at the top of her voice, finally looking him in the eye.

'Exactly,' said Don Pedro, turning round to walk out of the yard. 'I'm going to get Esperanza. I'll make her look splendid for you.'

So now the family could really start preparing for the festival.

Pancho and Antonio were back from the village square with the pesos they had earned from cleaning many shoes that morning. Their mother sent them out again to buy hair ribbons and shoe laces to give the final touches to the costumes which the family would wear that day.

Pepita and her mother and grandmother prepared and cooked food. Father packed everything very carefully into back packs for each person to wear. He also rolled up blankets for the night so everyone would have something to sleep in.

The smaller sisters played games in the yard in between running round to Don Pedro to see what he was doing to Esperanza.

At twelve o'clock, as Pepita was grinding the last of the chiles to make sauce, Maria came running into the yard.

'Is it really true, is it really true,' she shouted breathlessly. 'Is your grandmother really going up the mountain on Esperanza?'

News travels very quickly in Tepingo and Pepita wasn't a bit surprised that Maria already knew. She nodded proudly at her friend.

'Oh, Pepita, she is so lucky, I wish my grandmother could go too.'

'Can't she go on your donkey?' asked Pepita.

'No, the donkey we have isn't as surefooted as Esperanza, and anyway my grandmother is not well enough to go. She says not only is Esperanza a very special cow, but your grandmother is a very special person, and that she will have to go for all the old people in the village who cannot go, and they will be very proud of Dona Marcela.'

The two girls looked at each other shyly. Pepita was proud of her grandmother and sad for Maria's grandmother, and for all the other grandmothers who couldn't go.

The sun was very high now, and very hot, and all the animals were resting in the shade. The band had stopped playing and the musicians were resting in the village square. The smell of food hung over the village. Delicious food which would be carefully carried up the mountain for the great feast around the pyramid.

Into the midday peace ran Pancho and Antonio waving the ribbons and laces they had been sent to buy. They started tying up the two girls who shrieked and struggled to get free.

Pepita's mother appeared and clapped her hands briskly.

'Now stop that, you boys. Come along, children, it's time to start getting ready. Maria, run along home, you will be needed there, and Pancho and Antonio start washing.'

Finally it was time to get ready!

24

Maria ran off home and Pancho and Antonio groaned at the prospect of washing.

Soon there was such a frenzy of washing and cleaning and brushing that there wasn't time to think up any more tricks.

Even the little girls who were not going to climb the mountain had new dresses, and they were looking forward to their own party, especially as Don Pedro would play his flute so they could dance.

Nobody noticed that Grandmother had disappeared.

At half past one the family lined up outside the house for mother to inspect them all.

Father looked magnificent in his white suit and navy blue cape which was embroidered with the golden jaguar. He wore a heavy wide sombrero and stood with his hands on his hips, looking at Mother in her loose white dress embroidered with red and yellow flowers and wearing a fringed turquoise shawl over her head to keep the sun off. She looked very beautiful.

Pancho and Antonio wore white suits too, with red embroidered arm bands and special straw sombreros.

Pepita felt very grand in her own prettily embroidered white dress, and her mother had plaited ribbons of many colours through the pigtails of her long black hair. She was so excited she couldn't stand still and with the little girls she jumped around all over the place.

'And where is Grandmother?' asked Antonio wriggling uncomfortably in his new suit.

But before anyone could reply the sound of Don Pedro's flute came wafting down the lane.

He walked into the yard playing a tune from the Revolution, and there prancing behind him, her head held high, came Esperanza. Bedecked with flowers and ribbons, she looked very splendid indeed, and on her back was a wooden seat with a high back full of comfortable little cushions and complete with a special safety belt so that Grandmother couldn't possibly fall off.

The family crowded round in delight to inspect Esperanza. The turkeys pushed in to make their own inspection and it was hard to tell who was the most pleased with all the attention, Don Pedro or Esperanza.

The only person missing was Grandmother, and amid the laughter and chatter nobody remembered to ask where she was until Esperanza gave one of her loud moos and tossed her head in the direction of the trees behind the house where the river runs.

There, walking towards them, wearing her own long white embroidered dress, a parasol over her left shoulder and Felipe the parrot perched on her right one, came Dōna Marcela.

She looked simply magnificent. The younger children had never seen her dressed in anything but black before and they stood in amazed silence as the men swept the hats from their heads.

Pepita watched her grandmother walking so sedately, feeling as amazed and proud as everyone else, but at the same time, out of the corner of her left eye she was keeping a wary eye on Esperanza.

Would Esperanza still object to being called crazy by Grandmother? Would she now throw a tantrum?

But Esperanza had a very forgiving nature, and now she set

26

off at a brisk trot toward Grandmother, who stood waiting for the amiable cow to approach her.

Father ran over and swept Grandmother up into the special seat and Esperanza made a trial walk around the yard while everyone cheered and the neighbours came running to look at the dignified couple. Accompanied of course by Felipe who had decided he was going up the mountain too!

'Now,' said Don Pedro, 'the rest of you, pick up your things and be off with you. We want you at the head of the procession not at the tail.'

And he picked up his flute and played the Jiminez family out of the yard while the little girls waved and cried, and the turkeys climbed into their favourite tree for a special, festival gobble.

Out on the road the whole village was on the move. Everyone cheered when they saw Grandmother and Esperanza, and Dona Marcela twirled her parasol and bowed to everyone she saw.

The road soon came to the foot of the mountain where a narrow rocky path began the winding route to the plateau on which the pyramid stood.

The village band went first so they would be there to play when everyone arrived. Their instruments gleamed in the sun as they walked sturdily ahead.

After the band followed the Mayor and the officials and the elders of the village, all carrying their masks which they would wear at the ceremony at the top of the mountain. The faces on the masks were the same as the animal faces carved on the pyramid.

And when those two groups were well on their way the villagers made way for Dona Marcela and Esperanza, with all the Jiminez family following behind.

Through the avenue of people the family walked, looking very splendid. Father played the drum to get everyone off to a good start.

As she stepped onto the rocky path, Pepita felt someone slip a hand into hers.

'I want to walk with you,' said Maria, and Pepita smiled happily at her friend.

And so the village was on its way to the top of the mountain to the pyramid which the ancestors had built.

People walked carefully, some stumbled, some were very quiet as they concentrated, and others sang. Everyone stopped for breath from time to time, and little by little the trees disappeared and the hot sun beat down with no shade on the path.

'Think how easy it will be in the morning when we come down,' said Pepita's father as he occasionally gave the girls a lift on his shoulders.

But no matter how hot the day, or how steep the path, Esperanza never looked tired for a minute and Grandmother sat comfortably among her cushions encouraging everyone with her parasol while Felipe fluttered about her.

'What an amazing lady,' the villagers remarked to one another as they struggled up the mountain. 'If she and Esperanza can make it, so can we.'

And finally, after three hours of walking, just as the sun was

beginning to go down, the procession turned a corner and there in front of them was the square building which was the pyramid.

Indeed they had arrived.

'We're here, we're here,' Maria just had enough breath to shout and she gave Esperanza a playful push which Grandmother did not appreciate.

Little by little the villagers, their costumes slightly soiled by the climb, straggled onto the plateau and collapsed in exhausted groups on the ground.

The brass band, which had been there long enough to recover its breath, played some cheerful tunes to freshen everyone up.

Standing at the entrance to the plateau, the pyramid behind him, was the Mayor who welcomed the weary villagers one by one.

And standing right beside him were not the village officials or the elders, but Grandmother and Esperanza.

Everyone who passed by stopped to pat Esperanza and greet Dona Marcela, and in return she gave each person a candle to use in the ceremony.

Half an hour later Pepita and Maria sat on the edge of the plateau and looked around them.

They had been exploring. They had found the pyramid was a square stone building as tall as a three-storey house. They had never seen a three-storey house because the tallest house in Tepingo only had two storeys so the pyramid seemed very tall to them.

It was covered with carvings of the faces of animals which used to live in the valley in the time of the ancestors. In those days each year was given the name of an animal and that is why this year the theme of the ceremony was the jaguar.

Behind the girls the women were preparing the food over small fires which was going to be eaten at the big feast to celebrate the festival of the ancestors. The food would give everyone the energy to dance after the long climb.

The men were discussing the arrangements for the ceremony and the children were scrambling over the pyramid which had steps built into two sides.

All over the valley below the two girls, the sunset was painting everything a very deep pink and as they watched it seemed as though the roofs of the homes in Tepingo were catching fire.

'Look,' said Pepita, nudging Maria, 'there is the market place and over there is where we stood looking up at the pyramid this morning.'

'Yes,' said Maria, 'and you didn't think you'd get your grandmother up here, did you?'

The girls giggled as they turned to watch Dōna Marcela finally being lifted off Esperanza.

Pancho and Antonio came wandering up.

'The pyramid's not as big as I thought it would be,' said Pancho kicking a stone over the edge of the plateau.

'But it was big enough for the ancestors to be able to see from for hundreds of miles, and know whether anyone was coming to invade the valley,' said Antonio who was pretty good at history.

'Do you mean somebody came up here every day to keep a look-out?' asked Maria, who thought one journey every six years was quite enough.

'Oh yes, people lived up here for days, and the ancestors

32

believed that when their people died, their spirits came up here to keep a watch over the village. That's why they built the pyramid. The ancestors thought this was the most beautiful place in the world,' Antonio said.

'It is,' said Pepita looking a long way into the distance. 'It is.' But she silently thought it would also be nice to see other places too.

But now the sun was dropping fast behind the mountains and the smell of food cooking on the fires made the children run to their families.

Soon everyone was sitting on the ground around the fires, eating tacos with their fingers, laughing and talking, or listening to the stories of the elders.

When everyone had finished eating the mayor climbed to the top of the pyramid and stood looking very impressive in his mask of the jaguar with his arms held up high.

The elders, wearing their jaguar masks too, made a circle around the foot of the pyramid and everyone gathered around to watch and listen.

The mayor spoke in Nahautl and although most people didn't understand the old language the people were very quiet as his words resounded around the plateau and the night wind carried the legends of the ancestors out into the valley. He talked for a long time and Pepita shivered a little. It was very eerie hearing those words and the wind in the dark. She and Maria held hands tightly.

When the speech was finished everyone covered their heads with shawls or sombreros and lit their candles.

Then all the villagers, and all the people from the other

villages and the people who had come from the big city, followed the Mayor and the elders in a slow procession three times around the pyramid.

Those who could speak Nahautl chanted special words as they walked and Pepita thought it sounded like humming so she hummed along too.

Nobody noticed the wind, they walked close together and everyone felt close together. The candles gave a magic light which caught the faces of the animals carved on the pyramid and cast reflections on the special costumes.

'They look as though they are moving,' whispered Maria as the girls watched the lights playing on the animal carvings.

Finally the procession around the pyramid ended and everyone moved into a circle in the middle of the plateau. When one circle closed another one formed around it until all the people were standing in circles inside circles holding hands.

The candles had finished and the fires had gone out. There was no light now except for the stars above.

'How close they seem,' thought Pepita looking up at the sky. 'And how many! I've never seen so many.'

Suddenly huge torches of fire were lit around the edges of the plateau. Flaming torches casting light over everybody.

A figure ran into the middle of the circles dressed completely as a jaguar dancing the dance of the jaguar and shaking rattles in his hands as he danced. The people stood spellbound, watching him.

Then, as the dance was finishing, into the middle of the circles marched the village brass band playing the best music Pepita had ever heard them play. Everybody began to dance and jump and weave around, laughing and shouting and clapping their hands.

Esperanza was there of course, Right in the middle of everybody. She wasn't much good at dancing but her great body swayed in a sort of rhythm, scattering flowers and ribbons everywhere and Pepita saw her grandmother laugh until the tears ran down her face.

The dancing went on for hours and hours. Long into the night. There was more to eat, other groups of musicians joined in the playing and firecrackers exploded all over the plateau and the valley.

Pepita and Maria, Pancho and Antonio danced and played, ate and laughed until their legs were aching and their stomachs were so full they could hardly move.

During the dancing Pepita found her grandmother sitting on a rock and she sat down at her feet to rest.

'Are you happy you came now, Little Grandmother?' asked Pepita.

'Yes, of course I am,' said Dona Marcela hugging her granddaughter hard. 'And I think Esperanza's having a very good time too!'

They both laughed as they watched Esperanza's great swaying body.

'But Grandmother,' Pepita looked up into the old lady's eyes, 'where are the ancestors?'

'They're here little one, I feel them, they are with us. Now you go back to the dancing.' And Pepita left her grandmother sitting by herself with a smile on her face.

Much later the dancing came to an end, the torches went out

and each family made another little fire so everyone could lie down around it and sleep under their blankets until dawn came.

The sky was very dark now the stars had completely disappeared. Pepita and Maria settled down beside each other.

As they were arranging their blankets, Pepita felt a big bump.

Esperanza had arrived and flopped down beside her falling straight off to sleep. She was exhausted!

The two girls laughed and laughed. They didn't even care that Esperanza was blocking the heat from the fire.

'What a day!' said Pepita tugging her blanket out from underneath Esperanza.

'Yes, I can't wait another six years for the next one,' Maria said sleepily.

And as Pepita began to close her eyes, out of the silence which had fallen over the plateau, she thought she heard music.

She propped herself up on one arm and listened carefully.

The music was coming up from the village. It was Don Pedro's flute. He had said she would hear it, and there it was! He was playing a lullaby which the ancestors used to play on their flutes.

Beside her, Esperanza opened one eye and cocked an ear. She was listening to her master's music and watching Pepita.

On the other side of the fire Grandmother was also watching Pepita. Her mouth moved as she watched her granddaughter.

'You made this day possible, thank you.'

Pepita felt very happy and very proud of her grandmother and Esperanza.

She snuggled up against the friendly cow and fell into a very deep sleep.

THE · CARNIVAL · THIEF

Pepita was sitting in class waiting for the bell to ring for the end of lessons.

She didn't usually sit there waiting for the bell to ring, she quite enjoyed school, really, and it was better than doing the chores at home. Besides, she hoped her parents would let her go to secondary school one day when she was old enough.

But *who* could sit in class on a day like today? Through the open windows of the village school came the sounds of at least seven brass bands practising music, while somebody tested a loudspeaker system and the voices of a great number of people added to the amount of noise. Apart from all the noise came the smell of cooking, delicious smells from many different kinds of foods.

Today was the day the carnival started. The village had a three-day carnival every year just before Lent, when the villagers would have a big *fiesta* of dancing, music, song and special foods. The carnival was a last celebration before the forty days of Lent when there were no parties and everyone led a quiet life and ate simple foods until Easter arrived.

The first day of the carnival was always the most important one for the villagers and today the children would be allowed to finish school at twelve o'clock instead of two o'clock so that they could see the carnival begin.

Once the dancing started it went on for three days without stopping, day and night, and people from the city and from other villages, even people from overseas came to the village to join in the dancing and other festivities. When the dancers from other villages were tired they just dropped on to the floor of the village square and went to sleep until they were refreshed enough to go on dancing! It was a crazy time in Tepingo and Pepita and all the other children loved it.

So this morning, as they all sat wriggling in their seats, the children were thinking of the dancing competitions, the colourful masks and costumes which the dancers would wear and the funny plays which would be acted in the streets around the centre of the village. The dancing was the most important activity for the older people, who never seemed to stop, and so the children were able to get on with their own activities during the carnival. There were special carnival sweets, and costumes to wear as well as special games to play and all those people to meet and talk to.

This year, for the first time, there would also be a funfair. The funfair had been specially brought from the city. There had never been one in the village before and the children had talked of nothing else for weeks. Only Toni Perez had ever been to a funfair. He had been to stay in the city and when he came back he told all his schoolmates about his visit to the funfair in the big park and especially about the thrill of the big wheel. So there was great excitement in the village when the children saw the big wheel being put up that morning as they were on their way to school.

Pepita looked at her friend Maria who was sitting beside her and they pulled faces at each other. The teacher was still going on about the same piece of history as though there were nothing at all special about the day. She came from the city and Pepita thought she probably didn't understand the ways of the village.

Finally the bell rang. The teacher closed her book and dismissed the class. Pepita and Maria were among the first to reach the door when they were stopped by the sound of Senorita Ortiz calling their names.

'Pepita and Maria! Now you know it is your turn to clean the classroom today,' she told them crossly.

They looked at each other. It was true, they had completely forgotten! Every day two pupils had to sweep the floor, dust the desks and chairs and wash the blackboard, as well as put away all the books. Tepingo was too poor to afford a school caretaker.

By the time they had finished their cleaning all their classmates had disappeared and Pepita and Maria ran down to the market place to see what they were missing.

They were amazed at what they saw. Where, four hours ago there had just been a square beginning to fill up with people, now it was difficult to recognise the place where they usually came to do the shopping for their families. A platform had been set up at one end for the judges of the dancing to sit on, the funfair had been finished and was already working, the village musicians were already winding through the crowds of people playing the dance music, the food stalls were busy and the streets around the square were jammed with cars and people. The noise was terrific. Sometimes two bands would be playing the same piece of music but not at the same time and Pepita and Maria put their hands over their ears until they had got used to the unusual sounds.

But the most fascinating sight of all, of course, was the big wheel which towered over the village square. The girls couldn't take their eyes off it. It was *huge* and it had seats like buckets hanging at intervals around the wheel and it was already spinning although nobody was riding on it yet.

'I can't wait, I can't wait,' yelled Maria above the noise, hopping from one foot to another in excitement.

'Let's go and see,' Pepita yelled back, but before they could take a step forward both girls felt something very hard bump on their heads, and suddenly their hair, their faces, their eyes, their noses and their mouths were full of flour.

Loud laughter came from behind them and through the flour the girls turned to see Pepita's brothers, Pancho and Antonio, standing there with eggshells in their hands falling about with laughter.

It was all part of the carnival. Like other children in the village, Antonio and Pancho had been saving eggshells for weeks. They filled them with flour, stuck them back together and then painted the outsides in bright colours. It was part of the carnival fun to crack these over other peoples' heads, as well as shower people with confetti and put slimy jellies down their backs.

'We'll get you!' yelled Pepita as the boys started to run away.

'Oh no you won't,' yelled back Antonio. 'And Mother wants you at home.'

'Grrr. . .' was all Pepita could say in reply as she and Maria

41

rubbed the flour out of their eyes and hair, knowing they would have to do that quite a few times in the next few days.

'I suppose we'd better go home before we go to see the big wheel,' said Maria.

'I suppose so,' sighed Pepita looking sadly at the tempting big wheel. It seemed to her that life was full of chores which stopped her from doing the real things.

'I hope I find you here later,' said Maria, 'I'll have to bring all my brothers and sisters with me this afternoon.'

'I'll be looking for you,' Pepita said.

When Pepita walked into the yard which surrounded the little wooden house where she lived, she found her whole family in a state of activity.

Pancho and Antonio were letting off firecrackers, together with some cousins, and they were frightening the donkeys, pigs and turkeys; but as usual nobody stopped the boys from creating havoc.

Her four little sisters were banging on Father's drums and Grandmother was blowing up masses of balloons. Some for the girls and some to sell to the carnival visitors. Felipe, Grandmother's parrot was hiding in her lap because he was frightened of the sound of the firecrackers.

Mother was making mountains of tortillas to sell with beans and chicken stew at the carnival. Inside the house the two dogs were barking at the noise of the firecrackers, and outside the turkeys were scrambling into the trees, even though they didn't usually go there until six o'clock.

As Pepita walked through the gate, Torta the tortoise was

making slow progress out of this madhouse and she almost tripped over her. In the far corner of the yard, Father and Pepita's big cousin, Manuel, were very carefully touching up the paint on the masks they would wear for the dancing when it started properly.

The masks were very grand. They had real hair wigs glued on to them and very large noses which stuck straight out in front of them and then curled up at the end. They were painted in very bright colours and the faces looked funny and a little sad at the same time.

The masks were also very old. They had been in the family for many generations. The previous year a man from the city had offered Father a lot of money for his mask. Father had been most offended.

'The people of Tepingo do not sell their heritage,' Father had told the man.

'What's heritage?' Pepita had asked her father when the man finally went away.

'The traditions and possessions that have been handed down to us from our ancestors over many generations,' Father had replied.

Pepita thought that the little carved bowl which her grand-mother had given her must be part of her heritage, although she was not very proud of it; it was not nearly as magnificent as the masks.

This year, Father and Manuel would wear the masks with costumes made of satin and velvet which reached to the ground and had very wide sleeves. They were part of the dancing team which would represent the section of the village in which the Jiminez family lived.

The teams held competitions to see who could last longest dancing certain steps, or which team had invented the best dance this year, or which team danced the oldest dance in the best way. There were many competitions and they went on for three days and all the time, all the people who were not in the competitions, just danced all around the square, all around the teams, until it seemed like one big mass of movement which only the judges could sort out. It was an exhausting time, but it was very exciting. It was an honour to be asked to be part of a dancing team, and the family were very proud of Father and Manuel.

The women were never asked to join the teams although they joined in the dancing when they had time, between cooking and selling food or making sweets for the children.

Pepita had asked her mother why the women didn't form their own dancing groups and have competitions too.

'I think the women of Tepingo are much too busy to practise for competitions,' her mother had replied.

Pepita thought that was a shame.

Now her mother was calling to her from the wood fire where she was cooking.

'Pepita! Why are you so late?'

'It was our turn to clean the classroom,' replied Pepita, shooing some chickens out of the way and sitting down on the ground in front of the fire, to eat her lunch.

Her mother handed her a tortilla and Pepita filled it with beans from a bubbling pot. She put some chili sauce on the top and ate with her fingers without a plate, rolling the tortilla around the rest of the food so that it looked like a sausage and the beans couldn't fall out. The Jiminez family didn't very often eat meat, except for special occasions when they ate one of their own animals. They couldn't afford to buy meat, so mostly they ate beans and tortillas which were corncakes. Sometimes they ate fish from the river when someone was lucky enough to catch a few, and sometimes they ate eggs. That was all, they almost always ate the same thing every day. Today Pepita's mother was also cooking a chicken stew, but she was going to sell that at the carnival to make money.

Pepita found she was hungry even though she was excited and as she ate she asked her mother when she could go to the carnival.

'Now, Pepita, I've told Antonio and Pancho already. You are to watch the procession from here as it goes past the gate.'

Mother saw Pepita pull a face.

'Oh yes,' she insisted, 'you must stay here to watch the procession; there are too many people milling around in the square at that time, you will get smothered. When the procession has passed it is easier to move about, then you can go down to the square, but you must stay on the edges, there are too many people dancing in the middle. Oh, and you and Antonio are to take some of my embroidered belts to sell to the visitors. Pancho will take his shoebox and clean shoes. We must all try to make as much money as possible while we have the chance. Grandmother will take care of the little girls.'

'SELL!' Pepita exploded. 'Oh, Mother, today!'

'Yes, Pepita, if you are old enough to go to the carnival on your own, you are old enough to do something useful while you are there, and you and the boys all need new clothes for school.'

She was right of course. There was never much money in the Jiminez family. Father worked as a farm labourer on a big farm, but he didn't earn much money even though he worked very long, very hard hours. Sometimes there wasn't enough work for him to do on the farm and he was sent home. On their own very small piece of land, he and mother worked hard growing food, taking care of the few animals they could afford to look after and making things to sell whenever they could. They were always working, and there was never quite enough money for all the things a big family needed.

Pepita's mother embroidered beautifully, and she made small belts and bags to sell to visitors. She also had very good handwriting, and the people who couldn't read and write in the village came to her house and paid her a peso to write their letters or to ask her to help them read important papers. Every little helped and even the children had to find ways of making money when they weren't in school. Pepita had got used to the idea, but she didn't like it.

Grandmother noticed Pepita's gloomy face and winked at her over the top of a balloon. She tied the balloon up and bounced it towards Pepita. As she reached for another one she took a deep breath, but instead of blowing up the balloon, she burst into the carnival song at the top of her voice. Grandmother still had a very strong voice.

Although the carnival was now held at Lent, it had been a ceremony long before Christianity came to Mexico. The ancestors had had a similar event which lasted several days with plenty of dancing. The songs which had been sung in those days had survived and been handed down through the generations. Grandmother knew most of those songs. She sang in the ancient language, although most people in Tepingo sang in Spanish these days. Father knew some of the words of this song, and he started singing along with Grandmother. Manuel reached for the drums and accompanied them while the four little girls got up and put their arms around each other and started the carnival dance. Pepita, her brothers and cousins joined them, and mother clapped her hands in rhythm with the dancing.

The animals stopped being afraid. Felipe swooped around the dancers and the turkeys gobbled as though they too were singing. Behind her, Pepita heard a clatter of hooves and sure enough Esperanza, Don Pedro's cow, had come in from next door to push her way into the dancing circle.

Esperanza could never resist a dance. Over the fence, Don Pedro had started playing his flute to keep in tune and people passing in the street popped their heads round the gate to watch the Jiminez family start off the carnival.

Gradually the family became aware that the tune they were dancing and singing to was being played by more than just the drums and flute. A whole brass band could be heard as well!

'The procession,' shouted Mother. 'It's started, the band is marching down the street!'

Father and Manuel scurried to put on their costumes and then ran out into the street to join their dancing team. Mother had made all the children shiny masks and hats to wear to the carnival. Pepita and Antonio had decided they would paint their faces to scare everyone they met, but first Pepita had to run and put on some old clothes. No use wearing good clothes to the carnival – there were too many tricksters about.

As she ran to the house, Pepita caught sight of the powder eggs which the boys were taking to the carnival. She grabbed two and ran back to break them over her brothers' heads before she ran away laughing at their surprise and anger.

The boys were furious. They didn't have too many eggs left and they certainly hadn't expected to have two of them broken over their own heads.

A short time later, Pepita and Antonio, covered in paint and wearing masks and hats, tagged on to the end of the procession where everyone was splendidly dressed in costumes and masked, dancing their way to the square. The children were carrying straw bags stuffed with Mother's embroidery, and as Mother watched them dance happily away she wondered whether they would remember to sell anything.

The village square was a sea of moving people. Pepita and Antonio grew dizzy looking at the rows of bobbing heads dancing in time to the music, they laughed and laughed.

'It looks like waves on the sea,' shouted Antonio above the noise.

'Yes, it makes you seasick to watch them,' Pepita laughed back.

'How do you know, you've never seen the sea?' yelled Pancho from behind them, on the look out for customers.

'Know-all,' yelled back Antonio and Pepita together.

Pancho had been to the sea to visit an uncle and they had been very jealous when he went.

'Race you to the big wheel,' yelled Antonio setting off around the edge of the square to reach the funfair.

'Hey! Wait for me,' yelled back Pepita, running after him. When they arrived under the big wheel, they dumped their straw bags on the ground and looked up at the amazing contraption for a very long time. It was HUGE! It was spinning round and a lot of city children were shrieking away, obviously having a great time riding on the wheel.

Nothing else in the funfair, not the roundabouts or stalls with prizes or a giant rocking horse, nothing, compared with the big wheel.

As it came to a stop, Antonio turned to Pepita. 'Let's go and ask how much for a ride,' he said and they shuffled over to the man who worked the wheel.

'How much for a ride?' asked Pepita.

'Five pesos,' he replied.

FIVE PESOS! Pepita and Antonio looked at each other in horror. They felt as though they had just been robbed. Each of the children had saved their cents carefully for weeks to go to the carnival, but the most they had been able to save was two pesos. How on earth would they find another eight pesos for the two of them to ride on the big wheel? They looked up at the wheel in dismay.

Antonio and Pepita didn't often want something so badly that it made them cry, but every child in Tepingo had wanted a ride on the big wheel which Toni Perez had talked so much about.

'Maria's going to cry when she finds out about this,' Pepita said, choking back her own tears. Antonio couldn't say anything, he was too near to crying.

They gazed up at the wheel, which was beginning to move again, and as they watched they didn't notice a woman watching them. She was an American woman, a tourist on holiday in their country. She understood a little Spanish and she had watched their faces as they had talked about the price of the rides.

The woman walked over to Antonio and Pepita. 'How much are those beautiful belts?' she asked.

'Five pesos each,' answered Pepita, hardly looking at the woman, she was still watching the wheel in disbelief.

The woman picked out a belt from each of their two bags.

'Here, I'll take two, that's ten pesos, isn't it?'

'Yes, thank you,' replied Pepita, taking the money and tucking it inside her blouse where she always kept her money.

The woman watched her in surprise. 'But surely you can use the money to have a ride on the big wheel now, can't you?' she asked, smiling at Pepita.

Pepita looked at the woman properly for the first time. 'But this money is for our Mother,' she explained. 'She will need it at home.'

The woman blushed bright red, it hadn't occurred to her the children had to work to help support the family. She turned away and walked over to the man who ran the big wheel. She bought two tickets for a ride and walked back over to Pepita and Antonio.

'Now, you go and get on that wheel,' she told them.

Pepita and Antonio couldn't believe their ears! The woman

had to push them forward because the wheel was getting full. They were so shocked they didn't even have time to say thank you before they found themselves being strapped into the wooden seats with a bar put down in front of them to stop them from falling out. They saw the woman walking away into the crowd of dancers, looking for pictures to take with her big camera.

'I can't believe what happened,' said Pepita.

'Neither can I,' said Antonio. 'It was very nice of her.'

'Yes, it was,' replied Pepita and then she looked grim. 'But people shouldn't be made to pay such ridiculous prices.' Antonio agreed with her.

As more people got on to the seats on the wheel, they found themselves moving towards the top, and soon there they were, right at the very top of the wheel where they could see the whole market place, most of the village and much of the land beyond.

'It's almost like being up at the pyramid, you can see so far away,' breathed Pepita, very excited.

'Look at all those people,' said Antonio, pointing. 'Hey, look, there's Pancho cleaning shoes. Hey! Pancho Hey!'

'Don't be silly, he can't hear you. But look over by the bandstand in the middle of the square, there's Father, can you see him?'

'Oh yes, he's talking to the Mayor, but why has he taken off his mask and where is it?' Antonio was craning almost too much out of his seat in order to get a better look.

'Sit down!' Pepita shouted at her brother. 'The mask is down there beside his feet, he was probably too hot and took it off to get some air.'

Just then the wheel jolted a little to let the last passengers get in, and at the same time Pepita let out a loud yell and clutched Antonio who was settling down properly again.

'*Antonio, look!*'

'For heaven's sake, Pepita the wheel hasn't started turning yet and you're already . . .'

'*No look!*' Pepita's voice sounded really desperate now. 'That man in the blue shirt and trousers who was standing behind Father. He's just taken the mask and moved off and Father hasn't noticed.'

Pepita was wriggling about in a state of agitation.

'Oh no,' yelled Antonio, waving his arms frantically in Father's direction. But of course it was no use, his Father didn't know he was at the top of the wheel, and he *still* hadn't noticed that the mask was gone.

'Watch that man, watch where he goes, he seems to be working his way through the dancers.' shouted Pepita and then she bent her head down towards the man who operated the wheel. 'Hey! please we want to get off, please can you bring us down, please; it's very important.'

She was waving and shouting as hard as she could but the man below had started the motor which worked the big wheel and he couldn't hear her. All the other passengers were looking at her, they obviously thought she was scared and wanted to get off. A second later the wheel began to move and they were trapped on the long ride which they had longed for so desperately and which was now to be so miserable.

'I've lost sight of him,' sobbed Pepita in despair.

'Hold tight, we'll find him, just try to think of things that we can do,' said Antonio, trying to be brave.

Round and round they went, with grim faces, gripping on to the bar which held them in, not noticing anything, not feeling anything about the ride, just worrying about the theft of the mask and wishing desperately they could get off.

'That man looks as though he comes from the city,' said Pepita. 'It could have been the man who offered Father all that money last year.'

'Poor Father,' sighed Antonio, looking out over the blur of people and trying to see whether his Father had noticed the theft yet. But the wheel was travelling too quickly and there were just too many people down there.

The two of them felt as though the wretched wheel would never stop.

'When we get off,' said Pepita, 'We'd better start looking for that man ourselves. There's no point in trying to find Father. He'll know by now and the mayor will have sent men to look for the thief. We know what he looks like, we'd better look for him ourselves.'

'How?' asked Antonio.

'Well, he seemed to be heading for the dancers, he was probably trying to lose himself in the crowd for a while until he felt it was safe to get away.'

'Yes, and then he would probably head for the cars at the entrance to the village to go back to the city,' added Antonio.

'Yes,' Pepita agreed, 'so if we go in from this corner and work our way through to the other side of the crowd we might find him doing the same thing. If we don't he'll probably be moving to the cars by then.'

'Anyway, we'll have to go through the crowd, even the edges are jammed now, but it would take ages trying to go round the edges, the village is already so full,' Antonio said. 'Better get out one of Mother's belts in case we have to tie him up. Put one round your neck, just in case.'

Pepita was very doubtful about being able to tie up a grown man, but she put a belt round her neck anyway.

The suspense of waiting for the wheel to stop was dreadful. But gradually they felt it slow down and then they had to wait for their turn to get off. As soon as the bar in front of them was released they were off, and pushing their way into the crowd.

There were bands everywhere, and children and adults jumping up and down in the carnival dance, forming lines which wove in and out of other dancers and then breaking up and forming other lines. The noise was deafening.

Pepita and Antonio tried to push their way through the lines of dancers, but progress was very slow, they didn't recognise anybody to ask for help because everyone was wearing masks, and nobody recognised them because of the paint on their faces!

'Try and keep close!' Pepita yelled at Antonio.

'I'm trying, I'm trying o–o–owwwwww,' Antonio groaned back in pain as a dancer landed heavily on his foot.

At the same moment a powdered egg landed on Pepita's head and she burst into tears as she was momentarily blinded and lost sight of Antonio. It felt dreadful being pushed and pulled by that thick throng of dancers when everything was so terrible anyway.

'Antonio, where are you?'

'I'm here, little sister, I'm here,' Antonio grabbed her and she saw he was crying from the pain of his foot as well.

'It's no use, this is hopeless,' he said, wiping Pepita's face with one of the belts as the dancing crowd still jostled them.

'The only way we're going to get through is by dancing ourselves,' said Pepita. 'This pushing and pulling is no use.' Her voice was getting hoarse from shouting against the music.

'Link arms with someone and start a line going across the square, keep it going across the square. We're good dancers; people will want to dance with us,' Antonio yelled.

Surprisingly, and despite Antonio's hurt foot, it worked.

They linked arms together, grabbed the people beside them, and in next to no time twelve people had formed a line which was crossing the square diagonally and which was successful in keeping together. One of the smaller bands realised what they were doing and started to follow them with their music and more and more people joined them so that the line was beginning to spread out across the square. It was attracting a lot of attention from other dancers because Antonio and Pepita had set such good standards.

Pepita and Antonio were so busy dancing and moving the line across the square it was difficult to look around for the thief!

They did see their cousin Manuel, with his mask under his arm, looking desperately around him. They knew he was looking for the thief, but they didn't have time to stop and talk to him.

Neither Pepita nor Antonio had time to look up and see their father standing on top of the village hall building, looking at the crowd through the mayor's binoculars, searching to see if he could spot his mask.

Most of the people in the dancing line were wearing masks; some people were wearing the whole Tepingo costume, others were just wearing masks, either paper masks or wooden ones.

As Pepita and Antonio got more used to the bobbing up and down movement of the dancing, they started to look around them. Pepita's arm was still linked through Antonio's. She turned her head to look at her brother's other partner, who was wearing a Tepingo mask. She let out a gasp, but immediately turned it into a cough and turned her face forward again. For there, with his arm linked through Antonio's was the thief himself *wearing* Father's mask.

Poor Antonio was so busy looking at the crowd in front of him he hadn't noticed the dancer beside him. Everyone else was so wrapped up in the movement and the music of the carnival dance they hadn't noticed the man in city clothes, wearing one of the most famous masks in all Tepingo.

What could she do? With all this noise she couldn't whisper to Antonio. If she shouted the man would hear and the line was already beginning to get close to the corner where he could take off and head for a car. There wasn't much time left. She had to act fast. But how?

Anything was better than nothing, so she decided to act as best she could.

'Get ready to kick that man beside you,' she said turning her head and reaching as close to Antonio's ear as possible.

'Can't hear you,' Antonio yelled back.

'GRAB THAT MAN BESIDE YOU!' Pepita shouted moving forward out of the line as she yelled.

Fortunately Antonio was quick enough to put out his leg and make the man stumble, but Antonio fell over and Pepita had to take a flying leap over her brother's body to catch the man's legs

and bring him to the ground before he could run. Within seconds Antonio was on the man's back, had grabbed his arms and tied him up with one of Mother's belts. The man was shouting in pain as Pepita pulled off the mask and showed it to the astonished crowd of people who had stopped dancing and started to form a circle around the little group.

'This is my father's mask,' Antonio yelled.

'This man is a thief,' yelled Pepita. The dancers in the immediate area wanted to know what was happening and why they were sitting on the tied up man. Suddenly Manuel pushed his way through the crowd.

'Well done, you two,' he said, pulling them off the man's back and hauling him to his feet. He shouted at someone in the crowd to go and get the mayor. There was no police station nor were there any police officers in the small village of Tepingo, so the mayor would have to make the arrest.

As the man was dragged to his feet, Pepita recognised him.

'That's the man who tried to buy the mask from my father last year,' she said.

'Yes, I know it is,' replied Manuel, who had been there last year when the man made his offer.

The man hung his head in shame as the crowd waited for the mayor to come. He didn't take long, and as a path cleared for him and two other village officers, Pepita and Antonio saw their father coming up to them. He gave them a big hug.

The mayor took charge of the thief and said very seriously to Pepita and Antonio, 'Come along with me. You will have to make a statement.'

Antonio and Pepita looked at each other with shock. What was a statement?

Father laughed at the expressions on their faces.

'Come along, you two,' he laughed, 'it means that you have to tell the mayor everything that happened so that he can write it down and present it as evidence to the court after the man has been charged with theft.'

When they got to the village hall, Pepita and Antonio found their family and friends and schoolmates had already heard the news and were there to cheer them. Maria showered them with confetti and the little girls ran up with sweets to give them.

The thief was locked in a cell to wait for the police from the nearest town to come and take him away to court.

The mayor sat down at his desk with Father on one side of him and Manuel on the other. Antonio and Pepita sat on chairs in front of the desk and they told the mayor everything that had happened. Even about the American woman who had paid for their tickets for the ride on the big wheel where everything had started.

When they had finished, the mayor, with a solemn expression on his face, told them to sign the paper he had been writing their evidence on. Father watched them proudly as they put their names on the paper. It was the first time they had written anything which wasn't school work.

Finally the mayor smiled for the first time.

'You have done well,' he said. 'Tepingo is proud of you. What can I offer you as a reward?'

Antonio and Pepita looked at each other. 'Another ride on the big wheel, we didn't enjoy the last one,' Antonio said for them both.

But Pepita was quiet, she looked very serious.

'Well Pepita,' said the mayor smiling, he knew Pepita's serious looks and what they meant. 'Have you lost your tongue? You can ask for something different you know.'

'No, I would like another ride too. It's just that . . .' Everybody was watching and wondering what she was going to say.

'Well, I only want another ride if you, as mayor, make the

wheel owner change his price from five pesos to two pesos for rides for children. His prices are too high for the people of Tepingo, only the city children can afford five pesos.'

There was silence in the office. Father looked shocked and Manuel looked out of the window. Antonio held his breath and the mayor looked very, very serious.

The clock on the wall gave a loud click, and suddenly the mayor burst out laughing.

'Of course, you are right, the rides are too expensive, and I should have done something about it. Come on, the two of you, and I'll pay for the rest of that noisy crowd out there too!'

Ten minutes later Antonio and Pepita and their brother and sisters, cousins and friends had filled up the big wheel and were waiting for it to start. Waving to them from below were Mother and Father and Grandmother and the mayor and even the dancers in the square stopped to give them a wave.

As a special treat, Antonio was wearing Father's mask. It was already growing dark and the first fireworks were beginning to explode over the square.

Pepita looked at Antonio and he peered at her from inside the mask.

'Well, I suppose it was worth it after all, at least we got to go on the wheel twice,' he said, wriggling the mask from side to side so his eyes kept disappearing.

They burst out laughing and just then the big wheel swung right round and they were off on their ride. All the passengers let out a cheer.

Pepita felt on top of the world, and she still had two pesos for another ride!

GHOSTS · IN · THE · CONVENT

School had broken up for the summer holidays and Pepita was cross. Summer in Tepingo means the rainy season. For three months heavy rains fall during the afternoon and early evening. The roads become rivers and the fields become lakes.

Pepita always felt cross that the wettest time of the year came during the longest school holiday. In the rainy season everyone has to get up early to work while the sun shines.

Who wants to get up early during the holidays Pepita grumbled? And who wants to work during the holidays? But in Tepingo everyone works whether they like it or not.

For the rest of the year the village is dry and dusty and the water becomes a trickle in the river. People worry about the shortage of water, especially as most of the houses don't have water connected to them, and the villagers have to carry the water in buckets. Water is very precious in Tepingo. If the rains come late everyone looks very worried.

This year the rains came on time. Pepita thought it was such a waste being shut up inside every afternoon, where everything smelled damp and musty; but the rains were far too heavy to go outside.

She would have been happy to spend the time reading, but she had read everything she was allowed to read in the village library and her parents couldn't afford to buy books. So she was not only cross, she was bored as well.

As well as everything else, she and Maria had been given a very annoying task to do during the holidays, which made them both feel even more grumpy. Every day, at eleven o'clock, they had to set out to take food to their fathers and brothers who had been working in the fields since dawn.

By the time they had walked all the way there, waited for the men to eat their food, and walked all the way back, it had usually started to rain. So they would arrive home very wet and very cross.

'It's not fair,' said Pepita to Maria as they walked along one morning. They each carried two baskets of food and Pepita was kicking a stone along as she walked.

'I know,' sighed Maria, 'I wish something exciting would happen.'

'But nothing ever does,' said Pepita kicking the stone so hard that it bounced over the wall into Don Pedro's yard. Esperanza the cow gave a loud moo – sounding rather hurt.

'You hit Esperanza!' Maria cried out.

'Sorry, Esperanza, didn't mean to,' said Pepita peering over the wall.

Esperanza gave a softer moo when she saw Pepita, and started walking towards the gate which opened onto the road.

'No, you can't come with us!' Pepita called out. 'It's a long way to walk and Don Pedro will wonder where you are.'

Esperanza mooed very loudly in protest.

'Go back, Esperanza,' Maria shouted at the cow who had started to follow them.

Esperanza shook her head sulkily, but she turned round and went back.

'Even Esperanza's bored,' Pepita said.

'Yes,' sighed Maria.

It took a long time to get to the particular field where the boys were working that day, and when they arrived Pepita's brothers, Antonio and Pancho, were lying under the tree where they usually had their lunch.

'What took you so long?' asked Antonio.

'The baskets are heavy,' snapped Pepita. 'Anyway, why aren't you working?'

'What a temper,' laughed Pancho.

'Some people have an easy life, I must say,' replied Pepita irritably.

'Father went with some other men to sell things at the market, so we thought we would have an early break today,' Antonio said quickly.

'Come on, come on! Let's have some food,' shouted the impatient Pancho.

Pepita was furious at the boys' attitude but she decided not to start a fight. After all it wasn't much fun for them either, having to work in the fields all summer. (Even though they didn't have to carry heavy baskets of food.)

There weren't many men working in the fields that day, so when Maria's brothers Carlos and Hugo came over to eat, elderly Don Pepe came with them for company.

'Well, what a gloomy looking group you are,' he said as he

accepted a tortilla and beans from Pepita. 'What *is* the matter with you?'

'We're bored,' said Pepita dreamily, serving the food.

'Bored! but surely you must be glad to be free of school for a few weeks. I wish I could have such a long break.'

'It's not much fun in the rainy season,' said Maria.

'And anyway, all we do is work,' Antonio muttered.

'Well, I don't know! Considering the amount of imagination you six usually have, I'm surprised you can't find anything to do at all.'

'Like what?'

'Yes,' Pepita said carefully, looking at Don Pepe. 'Have you got any suggestions, Don Pepe?' She could see he had thought of a story to tell them.

Don Pepe was famous for his story telling. Pepita thought he must be very, very old because he seemed to have so many tales from the past. She had been listening to them since she was a very little girl. Don Pepe was almost as good as Grandmother at telling stories, but somehow Pepita thought that Grandmother had a little something extra.

'Well,' said Don Pepe, putting on his serious thinking face, 'you could always go ghost hunting.'

'GHOST HUNTING!' all six yelled at the same time looking at Don Pepe with alarm.

Don Pepe wrinkled his eyes and started to chuckle.

'Yes, that's what we used to do at this time of year when I was young.'

'Where?' Pepita demanded

'Why?' Antonio shouted

66

'How?' added Maria at the top of her voice.

All six were so excited they couldn't sit still or quiet. But Don Pepe knew he had an audience now, and the children realised they would have to settle down and listen to the story which he wanted to tell.

'Of course, we never found them,' chuckled Don Pepe.

'Found who?' Pepita was too impatient to wait for the whole story.

'The three headless soldiers. It is said they always come back at full moon in the month of August to haunt the convent.'

'Who were the soldiers?' Pancho asked. Pancho knew that Don Pepe liked people to ask him questions.

'Well, it's a long story . . .' Don Pepe saw Pepita's face fall. 'But I'll cut it short.' Pepita smiled at him.

'Many years ago, when I was a little boy, there was a revolution in this country. You have probably heard about it at school.' The children nodded. They had heard about it at school, many times.

'Well there was a lot of fighting around here in those days. In fact most of the people in Tepingo went to live in the caves in the hills for protection. Those who were too old or too young or too ill to go to the caves, went to the convent and the nuns tried to protect them. The convent has secret tunnels where the people hid when a battle was going on.'

'I've never seen the tunnels,' Pepita interrupted.

'Me neither,' said Antonio. 'But we've all played around the convent hundreds of times.'

'Ah!' said Don Pepe. 'So now you know how secret they are! You will have to look hard for them if you want to find them.'

67

Pepita and Antonio exchanged looks while Don Pepe continued with his story.

'One day, three soldiers who came from this village, came to warn the nuns that an army was approaching. The leaders were looking for any men, young or old who they could force into being soldiers to fight for them.

'The three soldiers were very young and very brave, they stayed to defend the convent while the nuns helped the people to hide in the tunnels. Everyone was very frightened.

'When the army arrived, the only people they found in the whole village were the soldiers. Of course, the soldiers were soon killed by the army's bullets as they tried to defend themselves.

'The leaders of the army were so angry that the soldiers had given the villagers time to leave the village, they chopped off their heads and put them up on the convent wall as a warning of what would happen if the army came back.

'That happened on the night of full moon in the month of August. Afterwards people said that every full moon in August, the headless ghosts came back to walk in the convent. A few years after the revolution the nuns left the convent and it was never used again. So when we were children we used to go looking for the ghosts, but to tell you the truth we never used to stay very long because we were too scared!' Don Pepe chuckled as he remembered his past and things that happened when he was a child.

'Well, I'd better finish off my work,' he said finally, 'it looks as though it's going to rain, I don't suppose your parents will be very happy that I've been encouraging you to hunt ghosts.'

The six were left looking at each other, thinking about Don Pepe's story.

'Shall we?' Antonio almost whispered, and the others knew exactly what he meant.

'Oh yes!' Pepita and Pancho answered at the same time.

'I'm too scared,' said Maria looking very frightened.

Her brothers laughed at her, 'You're always scared,' said Carlos. 'Come on, Hugo, we'd better get back to work.'

'Hugo looked at his brother in surprise. 'But aren't we going to plan the ghost hunt?'

'Later, come on!' said Carlos moving away.

Something in his brother's voice told Hugo that he had better not ask any more questions, so he got up and went back to work.

'Perhaps they're scared, too,' said Maria watching her brothers walk away.

'I wonder what's the matter with them?' said Pancho.

'Oh, never mind those two, let's make plans,' said Pepita impatiently.

'We can't now, we have to finish work,' said Antonio, 'but we can all take a look at the convent on the way home and you two can go to the library and find out from the calendar what date is the new moon.'

Everyone sprang into action; the boys hurried back to the fields before the rain started and the girls packed up the lunch things. Pepita skipped her way out of the fields and on to the road.

'Hey, wait for me!' Maria grumbled, not at all as excited as Pepita.

'Oh it's so good to have a *plan*,' said Pepita, jumping up and down with excitement. This was a very different Pepita from the bored girl who had left home that morning.

'How can you be so excited about going to see some scary ghosts?' Maria demanded.

'I've never been on a ghost hunt before,' said Pepita. 'And anyway, it's something to *do*! Imagine, if we do see the ghosts we'll be famous!'

'And exactly what will you do if you see them?' Maria asked.

'Ummm . . .' Pepita hadn't really thought about that. 'Well, we'll . . . umm . . . talk to them, I suppose,' she said.

'How can a headless ghost talk,' Maria demanded.

Pepita had no answer. Ghosts were strange things when you really thought about them.

'Ha!' shouted Maria, 'I bet you would run away!'

'No I wouldn't,' Pepita said crossly, but secretly she was worried about meeting three headless ghosts. What would they look like? What would they be doing? What would they think of a group of children who came looking for them? But then, she thought, they were brave, kind soldiers when they were alive so surely they would be kindly ghosts?

Pepita thought about the problem all the way to the convent building, and she didn't say a word to Maria who was obviously thinking about things too. Pepita didn't want Maria to think she was afraid.

The building was supposed to be closed up so that nobody could get in, but the doors had rotted and there was no glass in the windows so children could always find a way in.

Pepita thought it was a shame the big building was so wasted. She was sure the village could find a use for it if everybody thought very hard.

'Let's shelter inside from the rain,' said Maria.

'Yes,' Pepita agreed, 'And then we can look for the secret tunnels.'

'I really didn't know there were any secret tunnels until Don Pepe told us,' Maria said.

'Neither did I,' said Pepita, 'and we've been in here hundreds of times.'

The two girls went round the back of the convent and squeezed through a hole in the door they always used to get into the building.

Pepita went first and Maria followed. Just as Maria squeezed through into the gloomy, cool room she felt something brush her face and heard a loud flapping noise. She screamed.

'What's the matter?' Pepita ran back to her friend.

'Something attacked me! Something attacked me!' Maria shrieked, crying into Pepita's shoulder.

'Maria, it's only a bat, it didn't attack you, you frightened it, that's all. Be quiet. You don't want the whole village to know we're here do you?' Pepita tried to calm her friend but Maria was shrieking again.

'Something ran over my foot,' she yelled.

'It's a lizard,' Pepita told her, watching it scuttle away. 'I expect we startled it, or you did when you screamed. Why are you so scared? You've never been scared in here before.'

'It's the ghosts,' said Maria, solemnly wiping her eyes on the hem of her dress. 'I didn't know about the ghosts before.'

'But the ghosts don't come during the day and they only come once a year,' said Pepita.

'How can you be sure,' Maria wanted to know.

Pepita didn't know. She was just hoping that Don Pepe had been right when he had said that the three soldiers only came at August full moon.

'Maria, stop crying! If you don't want to come with me go home. I'm going to explore and see if I can find the entrance to the tunnels.'

Maria did stop crying. She didn't want to go home and so she decided to try and be brave like Pepita.

'All right,' she said. 'Where shall we look?'

'Everywhere!' said Pepita and they set off to explore.

The convent was built around a square. There was a garden in the square which had been a pretty and quiet place for the nuns to sit. All the rooms led into each other, one after the other, all around the square. Pepita and Maria wandered through the rooms, opening cupboards in the walls and moving the few pieces of rubbish which had collected over the years, even though the nuns had taken all their furniture with them.

It took Pepita and Maria quite a while to search the big rooms carefully.

'There's nothing here,' Maria said at last.

Pepita was touching a wall, feeling it all over hoping to find a secret button that would lead to an opening.

'There aren't any secret passages and there isn't a trap door, it's no use looking any further, Pepita,' Maria said. 'Perhaps Don Pepe was joking.'

'No, no I'm sure he wasn't,' Pepita said, flopping onto a stone window seat and looking out into the garden. She hoped they wouldn't have to ask Don Pepe to tell them, because he might have changed his mind about encouraging them to go on a ghost hunt.

Maria was talking to Pepita as Pepita looked out of the window, but Pepita was only half listening. Outside the rain had stopped for a little while. Pepita was watching a big yellow butterfly flutter about the garden.

In the middle of the garden was a small fountain. Once, water had run down the fountain in a cascade. Pepita watched the butterfly fly around the fountain and she imagined how it had looked when the water ran. The butterfly sat on a little handle in the fountain and, as she watched, Pepita suddenly had an idea.

She sat up and shouted: 'I think I've found it!' and before Maria could understand what was going on, Pepita was climbing out of the window and running through the weeds to the fountain.

Maria scrambled through the window too, and ran after Pepita. Pepita had climbed up onto the base of the fountain; she reached up to the small handle where the butterfly had perched. She turned it and suddenly disappeared from Maria's view! The fountain had split in half!

When Pepita had turned the handle, half the fountain, the piece on which she was standing, had swung around and there, on the ground, was a trap door!

Pepita's head came round the fountain and grinned at Maria!

'I told you!' she shouted. 'Of course, when the nuns lived here the water was falling all the time and so nobody ever noticed the handle. Isn't it clever, Maria?'

'How did you work it out,' Maria asked.

'I was watching a beautiful butterfly sitting on the handle and while I was watching I suddenly wondered why a fountain needed a handle.'

'You are clever, Pepita!' Maria exclaimed.

'Only sometimes,' Pepita said as modestly as she could. 'Now let's try and open the trap door.'

The two girls took hold of the large iron rings and pulled very hard. They tugged and tugged but nothing happened.

'I suppose it's such a long time since it was opened that it's got stuck,' Pepita said at last. They sat on the ground to recover their strength.

'Let's try one more time, and if we can't do it, we'll have to get the boys to help.' But she didn't want to have to ask the boys. She was proud of her discovery and she wanted to be the first to see the secret tunnels.

They pulled again, and this time the door came up just a little. 'Quick, fetch that stone!'

Maria got the stone and jammed it under the door so that it wouldn't fall back again. They pulled again and this time the trap door lifted right up.

'Hooray!' shouted Maria.

Pepita was already peering down below. 'There are some steps leading down,' she said. 'Let's go down and see.'

'It's dark down there,' said Maria, looking very scared indeed.

'Ay, yes it's dark,' Pepita agreed, not feeling quite so brave now. 'We'll need to buy a torch,' she said.

'You can buy one,' Maria said. 'Nobody's going to get me to go down there!'

Pepita looked at her friend's frightened face.

'You stay at the top and watch me, I'll just go down a few steps,' Pepita said, 'If you can't see me any more shout down and I'll come up.'

'All right,' said Maria.

Pepita put her legs over the side of the opening and stood up on the first step. As she moved down, her hand touched the wall, which felt wet and slimy from all the rain which had seeped through. She shivered, a funny smell came from below, and even with the light from the trap door she couldn't see very far.

A lizard ran over her foot, giving her a fright.

'Ugh! Lizard, how can you bear to live down here?' she exclaimed, but the lizard had scuttled away, just as frightened as Pepita.

'What did you say?' Maria called anxiously from above.

'Nothing, it was just a lizard, Maria. Can you still see me?'

'Yes, but only just, I wish you would come up now.'

'Just a minute, don't be frightened, I'm all right,' Pepita's voice sounded excited.

Very dimly she could now see the last step and beyond that, there was what looked like a passage way. The wall was drier now and she pressed against it to keep from falling.

'I wish I had a torch,' Pepita muttered to herself, peering into the gloom in front of her. 'I'll have to think of a way of buying one.'

'Pepita, Pepita, come up, come up! I can't see you any more.' Maria's voice sounded desperate.

'Coming,' Pepita called, wishing she had a light to go further.

'What is it like?' Maria asked as Pepita climbed out of the trap door.

'It smells musty,' Pepita said, 'and it's very dark, but I could just see the beginning of a passage; I need a light to go further.'

'You wouldn't go through it alone would you, Pepita?' Maria looked shocked.

'Well, if I had a light and you were waiting at the top I would go a little way,' Pepita said. 'I have to think of a way to make some money to buy a torch.'

The rain started again as the girls put the trap door into place. They decided to run quickly to the small library, as Antonio had suggested, which was really just a room at the back of a store.

As they ran, Pepita thought again about Don Pepe's last words. It was true that their mother and father would probably not be too keen on the idea of a ghost hunt.

How could they get out of the house at night without attracting attention?

'Well, you two look as though you've been for a swim in the rain,' Senora Mendez laughed as the girls walked into her store. Senora Mendez took very good care of the village's collection of books, and she handed Pepita and Maria a towel to dry themselves before she would let them touch the books which they had obviously come to see.

The villagers were very proud of their book collection. There were nearly two hundred now, mostly second hand, given to the library by people who no longer needed them.

Pepita loved the small quiet room at the back of the store, which Senora Mendez had decorated with pictures and interesting articles from the magazines and newspapers which found their way to the village sometimes. She would often come during the holidays or at weekends, to read anything she was allowed to read. It was too noisy to read at home with all those people and animals!

'What can I do for you today?' asked Senora Mendez once the girls were dry and had entered the library.

'We'd like to see a calendar, please,' Pepita said.

'Oh! is that all? There's one on the wall over there. What are you looking for,' Senora Mendez asked, trying to be helpful.

'Oh, er, we were wondering when full moon comes this month,' said Pepita, while Maria kept her eyes on the calendar.

'You mean you got yourselves so wet just to find that out!' Senora Mendez gasped in surprise. 'You should have asked your grandmother, Pepita, you know she always knows dates like that. It's the seventeenth this month, the feast of the corn gathering. Don't you two remember anything about village festivals?'

Pepita's face lit up with joy. 'Thank you, Senora Mendez, thank you. Come on, Maria,' and she grabbed Maria's hand and rushed her friend out of the back door into the rain again.

'What are you so excited about,' Maria asked breathlessly when they were out in the muddy street.

'The feast of the corn gathering, Maria! How could we have been so stupid. Of course, it's usually held at full moon in August. It's when the rains are supposed to begin to stop and the corn harvest begins.'

Maria remembered now. 'Of course, so everyone goes out to the fields when the moonlight is bright, to light bonfires. And there's a service to bless the harvest and hope that it will be a good one and everyone cooks food over the bonfire and there is music and dancing.' She too was excited now. Both girls had forgotten that the festival was due. Families did not make great preparations for that feast, they just put aside a little extra food for a few days and then went with the rest of the village to the fields. They lit bonfires in each of the four corners of the field and the priests visited all the fields where there were people, to offer prayers for a full harvest. The people also believed that by lighting the fires

78

they were scaring off evil spirits from destroying their crops. Afterwards the families would cook and eat together and everyone would take along their instruments and sing and dance for a while.

Despite the rain pouring all over their faces Pepita gave her friend a big grin. 'That means everyone will be out that night, nobody will be at home and we can sneak away to look for the ghosts!'

'You can,' said Maria looking very serious. 'I'm staying in the fields to have fun, I'm not going to that creepy place at night looking for ghosts.'

'But you could stay at the top by the door while we go down, and warn the rest of us if anyone comes,' Pepita said.

'I'm not staying up there by myself,' Maria shook her head angrily.

'Well, bring someone else with you then,' Pepita replied sure that her friend really did want to take part in the adventure. 'But you must tell them to keep it secret.'

'I'll think about it,' said Maria beginning to run. 'I must get home quickly now, my mother will be furious I'm so late.'

Pepita's mind was full of plans as she walked home. 'It's the twelfth today,' she thought, 'so there are only five days to go. How am I going to find the money to buy a torch in only five days? And how much does one cost?'

She stopped off at the village hardware store and asked how much the cheapest torch cost.

'100 pesos,' said Don Tomas, not taking too much notice of Pepita because he was busy preparing a big order.

'100 pesos,' Pepita thought gloomily. 'That's a fortune.'

She was very bedraggled by the time she got home. Only the turkeys were outside to greet her as she walked into the yard, and they looked very sorry for themselves.

Grandmother and Pepita's sisters were inside the small house, sheltering from the rain. Smoke was coming from the chimney at the back of the wooden building. Grandmother always kept the smokey wood stove stoked up during the rainy season so the family could dry out. Nobody else was home yet, Pepita's mother had gone to sell in the market with her father.

'Well, you've been a long time today,' said Grandmother looking at Pepita suspiciously. 'And you're very wet and dirty.'

'Uhmm, yes,' Pepita agreed, not saying anything else. She knew her grandmother wouldn't ask her any questions about what she had been doing, not like her mother.

'Come and get warm by the fire,' Grandmother said. 'You can help me make tortillas.'

Pepita sat cross legged, gazing into the fire as her hands worked the dough into the round pancakes of corn which the family would eat in the evening. She sat quietly, trying to solve her problem.

The little girls were playing quietly for a change, and the silence was only broken by the squawks of Felipe the parrot. He was cross about the rain and having to stay inside so much. If he went out, his feathers got wet, and that made him even more cross! Every so often he took off from Grandmother's shoulder and flew noisily around the room, protesting loudly.

'All right, all right, Felipe!' Grandmother finally shouted at the parrot. 'We all know you're not happy about the rain, neither are we, now please be quiet!' Felipe flew back to Grandmother's shoulder and fixed his eye on the pile of tortillas which was growing beside the fire. Perhaps Pepita would sneak him one.

'Now, what's troubling you, Senorita?' Grandmother asked Pepita, fixing her with an inquisitive stare.

'Oh,' Pepita was startled. 'I was trying to think of a way to make some money.'

'Oh, you were, were you? For something special I suppose?'

'Yes, for something special,' Pepita and Grandmother looked at each other seriously for a while. Then Grandmother burst out laughing.

'Well, it must be very special if you don't want to tell me,' she laughed.

'It is,' Pepita nodded her head solemnly.

'Well let me think,' Grandmother put on her thinking face, she was thinking about how Pepita could make money. Pepita sat very still. Nobody disturbed Grandmother when she put on her thinking face, not even Felipe the parrot.

'When do you need this money?' Grandmother asked suddenly and Pepita's heart jumped.

She thought quickly. Today was Thursday the twelfth, so the seventeenth would be Tuesday.

'Tuesday,' she told Grandmother.

'That's the day of the corn feast,' Grandmother said, looking suspicious again.

'Yes, Grandmother, I know,' Pepita said.

'Hmm, I wonder what kind of devilment you children are planning?' Grandmother said sternly. But Pepita saw that Grandmother's eyes were twinkling and she almost burst out laughing herself. She really wanted to tell Grandmother because they usually shared all their secrets. But there was just a possibility that Grandmother might not approve of ghost hunting so Pepita felt she should keep this secret to herself.

'Well, the only thing I can suggest,' said Grandmother, slapping tortillas between her palms as Pepita watched her eagerly, 'is that you sell food for me at the *charreada* on Saturday and I'll let you keep half the money.'

'I didn't know you were going to sell food at the charreada,' said Pepita.

'Well, if I wasn't I am now, aren't I?' replied Grandmother, looking at the fire rather than at Pepita.

'Oh, Grandmother, I do love you,' squealed Pepita in delight, jumping up to hug the old lady.

'Well, I don't know whether you'll be so delighted on Saturday when you have all that hard work to do,' Grandmother said, but Pepita was too happy to think about the hard work; this was her chance to earn the money for a torch.

Besides, this would be the first time Pepita would be allowed to go to a charreada. Usually the boys went with their fathers. The charreada was a kind of rodeo where the men rode bucking horses or cows and did other kinds of tricks with animals. Pepita wasn't sure whether she agreed with this kind of sport. She thought it might be cruel, but she had never had the chance to go and see for herself.

When Antonio and Pancho came home they looked very gloomy.

'We went to the convent and we searched and searched, but

we couldn't find any secret tunnels.' Antonio whispered to Pepita so that nobody else would hear.

'Yes, I think Don Pepe was playing a joke on us,' Pancho joined in.

Pepita's heart leapt for joy, she had been much more clever than the boys.

'No he wasn't, I found them!' Pepita nearly shouted she was so excited. The boys were excited too and they all found an excuse to go outside while Pepita told her story. She told them about the date, too, and how it was the day of the corn feast.

'Good,' said Antonio. 'We'll be able to get away as soon as we've helped carry the food there and got the fires going.'

'Nobody will notice we've gone, there'll be too many people there, everyone will think we're off playing somewhere,' Pancho said.

'We'll creep away and get into the convent the back way,' Pepita said.

'It's going to be very dark there, we'll need a torch,' Pancho said.

'I've thought of that already,' said Pepita, but before she could explain her plan Pancho interrupted her.

'You've been doing a lot of thinking today, Pepita, you want to be careful.' Pepita decided to take no notice of her brother's teasing. There were more important things to talk about. She explained about Grandmother's idea to let her make some money by selling food at the charreada.

The boys didn't look too excited about that piece of news, in fact they looked a bit uncomfortable and kept quiet when she told them she would be working at the charreada.

83

'What's the matter,' Pepita asked, looking at the expressions on their faces.

'Oh . . . er . . . it's . . . er . . . just that we didn't know you would be there on Saturday,' Antonio said, looking a little embarrassed.

Why shouldn't I be there?' Pepita demanded.

'Uhmm, well you see,' Antonio began.

'Out with it,' Pepita shouted at them.

'We're riding bucking bulls in the junior event,' Pancho said quickly, realising it was no use trying to hide the truth.

'Oh are you? And why didn't you want me to know about that? Now I know why you didn't want me to be there. You don't want me to see you fall off the first time the bull bucks,' Pepita giggled and her brothers shifted uncomfortably, it was the truth and they couldn't deny it. No village boy in Tepingo wanted his sisters and other girls to laugh at him. Pepita thought boys were very silly about these things.

'Well, too bad, because I'm going to be there, and if I'm going to be responsible for buying the torch, and because I found the secret tunnels, I'm going to be the leader of this ghost hunt and I don't care what you or Carlos or Hugo say about it,' she said, enjoying this moment of triumph.

The boys knew better than to argue, they didn't want Pepita to make matters worse by taunting them all the time before they took part in the competition. But Antonio remembered something.

'Carlos and Hugo aren't coming,' he said. 'They were behaving in a very peculiar way, giggling all the way home and refusing to come to the convent with us. They told us they had something else to do that night and wouldn't be coming. I've never seen them act so strangely.'

'Oh well, we can do without them then,' said Pepita. 'I think I can persuade Maria to come if she comes with someone else, then she can stay at the top of the trap door and keep guard.'

'I don't think she'll want to do that, she'd be far too scared,' Antonio said.

'She might, anyway I'll ask her to help me on Saturday and see if I can persuade her.'

On Friday, Grandmother took out some savings from a tin which she kept buried in the ground behind the house. She and Pepita went to the market to buy the food for the next day and they spent the rest of the day cooking it. Grandmother usually made three times as much money as she spent when she made food to sell, so she made a good profit. Her food was good and word soon got round about where to buy good food.

Grandmother told Pepita she could keep half the profit for herself, so Pepita knew she had to make 200 pesos on Saturday so she could keep 100. She would have to work very hard to make 200 pesos.

At the market Pepita met Maria and told her about all the plans. She asked her friend to help her the next day.

'Yes I'll come tomorrow, but I'm not sure about Tuesday, I'll tell you tomorrow.' Pepita thought Maria looked a little nervous but she couldn't think why.

On Saturday, Maria arrived early to help Pepita take all the food down to the arena where the charreada was to be held.

When they arrived they had to pay two pesos to go in, but as they had arrived early they easily found a good place to set up their food stall. Pepita had carried firewood on her back and Antonio had brought Grandmother's metal cooking tray, so she set to work to make a fire which would heat the food.

The girls were so busy preparing the food and watching the horses, cows and bulls arrive, they didn't have time to talk about the ghost hunt. Two men arrived looking very splendid in black costumes with silver buttons and braids.

'Look, Pepita,' Maria cried out, 'real charros' costumes!'

Both girls stood up to admire the men who were so splendidly dressed and wearing large round hats with the brims turned up at the front. In Tepingo nobody could afford costumes like that. These men must have come from the city, and they would probably have magnificent horses too. Everyone around them was excited by the presence of these charros at the village charreada.

'Just think, Maria,' Pepita said, 'a few days ago we were so bored, and now there's so much happening! Which reminds me, are you coming with us on Tuesday?'

'Oh, um yes, Pepita,' Maria said looking a little uncomfortable. 'I can only come though if I bring my cousin Miguel.'

'Who says?' Pepita asked, looking at her friend suspiciously.

'Carlos and Hugo,' Maria said, fanning the flames of the fire so that she didn't have to look at Pepita.

'Why aren't they coming themselves?' Pepita demanded.

'Er, well, they've got something else to do so they asked Miguel to go with me. He's brave and strong and I'm not and I'd be frightened to stay there alone.'

Pepita didn't think Maria was telling her the whole truth, but just then a crowd of people came up to buy food and the girls became so busy they didn't have time to talk again.

Pepita was kept so busy, she didn't have time to go and see what was happening in the ring, but after a couple of hours she heard the announcement for the junior event and she slipped away to watch her brothers.

A bull was stamping his feet inside a metal pen. He was very angry about being shut inside the pen and he looked very fierce. The juniors were only supposed to ride the older bulls because they were not so fierce, but this bull looked very fierce indeed!

Antonio appeared and he climbed up the railings of the metal pen. Some men helped to lower him on to the back of the bull. They had pulled a rope round the bull's neck and Antonio took hold of it, looking very frightened.

When the gate opened, the bull rushed out, the crowd yelled and Antonio clung desperately to the short rope. But the bull was bucking its back and kicking its legs and showing just how annoyed it was to have somebody on its back. Very quickly, Pepita saw her brother thrown to the ground, shoulder first. The crowd roared with laughter and the bull ran off, glad to be free.

Pepita stayed to watch the same thing happen to Pancho.

'Stupid boys, stupid sport,' she muttered as she left the arena. 'No wonder they didn't want me to watch them. I hope they haven't broken any bones or they won't be able to go on the ghost hunt.'

At five o'clock, Pepita and Maria counted the money they had earned that day.

'Three hundred and eight Pesos, Maria, that's really good.'
Pepita gave her friend ten pesos for helping her. On the way
home Pepita bought the torch for the ghost hunt and some
batteries to put inside it and make it work. She had a little money
left over so she bought a length of rope.

'What's that for?' Maria asked.

'Well, as it's very dark in the passages I thought it would be a
good idea to tie the rope round our waists so we don't lose each
other!' Pepita replied and Maria laughed at her friend.

Time passed slowly for Pepita until Tuesday. She couldn't
wait for the ghost hunt to begin. Antonio and Pancho were
nursing their bruises but they hadn't broken any bones. They
arranged to meet Maria and her cousin at the back of the convent
at nine o'clock, just about the time the villagers would be
preparing their supper in the fields.

Tuesday seemed to Pepita to be the longest day of all! But at
last, night fell and Mother and Father called out to the children to
help carry things to the fields.

Pepita was ready first and she waited impatiently out in the
yard for the rest of the family.

'You're in a hurry, Pepita,' said Grandmother, who was next
to be ready.

'Yes,' said Pepita looking at Grandmother's twinkling eyes.

'Did you enjoy spending your money,' Grandmother asked
with a smile.

'Oh yes, thank you,' Pepita had hidden the torch and the rope
at the bottom of the food basket she was carrying.

'Good,' said Grandmother, knowing Pepita wasn't going to
tell her what she had spent the money on.

As the family set off along the road, Don Pedro and Esperanza joined them. Esperanza was wearing blue corn flowers around her ears.

'You look nice, Esperanza,' Pepita told the cow.

'Mooo,' Esperanza answered in a grateful tone.

'I think I'll have a ride if you don't mind,' Pepita said, and Esperanza stopped so that Pepita could climb on her back.

'Is this all right, Esperanza?'

'Mooo,' Esperanza replied, and the two friends set off contentedly towards the fields.

Antonio and Pancho had already helped to build the bonfires before the family arrived. There was a bonfire in each corner of the field and the air was full of smoke. The moon was full and bright and everyone could see each other very clearly in the moonlight.

'Did you remember the torch?' Antonio asked as soon as Pepita arrived.

'Of course I did,' she snapped at him. She had organised their ghost hunt, she had thought of buying the torch, she was the leader – how would she have forgotten the torch?

The three of them hopped from foot to foot waiting for the priest to come and bless their field. When he did come, he spent a long time talking and praying. It was nearly nine o'clock before he left the villagers to prepare their feast.

'Let's go,' Pepita whispered to Antonio and Pancho. They slipped away from the crowd of people, hoping nobody had seen them. They didn't notice Grandmother watching them from where she sat by the fire.

When they got to the back of the convent, Maria and Miguel hadn't arrived.

'Trust them to be late,' Antonio exploded, his voice sounding very nervous.

'It might have been hard for them to get away,' Pepita said feeling very nervous herself. She looked at Pancho and saw that his face was pale.

After a few minutes they saw Maria and Miguel running towards them. There was another girl with them, Miguel's sister, Leticia, who was in the same class as Pepita and Maria at school.

'We thought we might need an extra person if anything happened,' Miguel explained.

Pepita and her brothers looked shocked. They hadn't thought about anything happening to them.

'Oh Pepita, are you sure you want to do this? You look very nervous,' Maria said.

That shook Pepita into action!

'Of course!' she said, taking out her torch and flashing it on to the wooden door. 'Come on, let's get going.'

The six scrambled through the door and followed Pepita as she led the way through the rooms. They were very glad Pepita had thought of the torch. The rooms were full of bats and an occasional mouse scurried out of their way. They felt better being able to see these animals and where they were going.

Pepita led everyone out of the window from where she had first seen the handle with the beautiful butterfly resting on it. Then they crossed the courtyard through the weeds. Pepita climbed up on to the fountain and everyone watched as she pulled the handle and swung out of sight as the fountain split in half.

'Hey, that's clever,' Miguel shouted out.

'Ssh, be quiet, we don't want everyone to know we're here,' said Pepita peering round the fountain with her torch in her hand.

'Yes, you might frighten the ghosts,' Antonio added and everyone shivered in the moonlight. Maria took a good look around her but she couldn't see anything.

'I wish you'd hurry up,' she said. 'I'm ready to go home right now.'

Pepita and the boys sprang into action. The trap door opened more easily this time and Pepita, Antonio and Pancho tied the rope around their waists.

'I wish Carlos and Hugo were here,' Pancho said. 'Don't you want to come with us Miguel?'

'Er, no thanks, I'll stay here. Give a big yell if you're in trouble. I hope the ghosts are friendly,' Miguel replied, helping Pepita over the entrance to the steps.

'Be careful,' Maria said anxiously as she watched the three go down the steps.

Pepita's teeth were chattering and the hand which held the torch was shaking so much she couldn't point the light straight.

'What will we do if we see the ghosts,' Pancho whispered as they went down the steps. Nobody answered him.

'Let's keep very close together,' Pepita said when they arrived at the bottom of the steps.

She shone her torch in front of them and they saw a passage which turned gently to the left.

'Come on,' she whispered, and the three crept silently towards the bend, keeping close to the wall. When they turned the corner they saw that the passage twisted again, this time to the right. There was nothing in the passage and the three began to walk a little more bravely now.

'Round to the right,' whispered Antonio, 'keep your torch shining towards the ground, Pepita, we don't want to trip over.' Pepita had been shining the torch on to the walls, looking for the ghosts.

Pepita was first round the bend, leaving the boys for a moment in the darkness.

'Aaaagh! Aaaagh!' Antonio and Pancho heard a terrible scream from Pepita and felt a jerk on the rope. They fled round the corner almost falling over each other in the dark.

'Pepita, Pepita what's happened?' they yelled turning the corner to find their sister pale and trembling with her torchlight shining on a gruesome face.

Both boys jumped with shock. It was a terrible face! It had a hooked nose, slit eyes, a monstrous tongue hanging out of the mouth and long black hair straggling down the sides of the face.

But it wasn't human!

'It's a mask,' gasped Antonio with relief, taking the torch from Pepita and examining the face carefully. 'It's a Tepingo carnival mask, it must have been put there to frighten people off.'

'Well it certainly frightened me!' said Pepita, leaning weakly against the wall. 'Imagine turning the corner and coming face to face with that! It must be worse than the ghosts.'

'I expect they put one wherever the passage twists,' Pancho said. 'To scare people away.'

'Mmm, I wonder,' said Antonio, 'I'm sure I've seen that mask before somewhere, I think it might have been brought here recently.'

'Look,' Pepita said snatching the torch from Antonio's hand. 'The passage gets wider here, it's almost the size of a room. It must have been used as a storage room before the villagers started hiding down here. Then it narrows again back to a passage, but wider than before,' Pepita was walking through the room as she talked, the boys followed.

'Wait Pepita!' Antonio called. 'I'll lead the way this time. You shine the torch from the back, Pancho, so we can all see where we are going. We'll keep close together and turn the bends at the same time.'

They set off again, keeping close together. There was nothing in the wide part of the passage and it soon narrowed again to a twisty passage. They found three more masks, one at every bend, but they weren't startled now, they expected them to be there. Then they came to a circular room which seemed to be the last room. Pancho shone the torch over the walls.

'No secret doors, it's all stone,' he said.

'Mm, it's cold in here,' said Antonio and shivered. 'It was a cold place for the people to hide.'

'So,' said Pepita, 'no ghosts, only masks.'

CLANG!

Just as she finished speaking a loud clanging noise came rattling down the passage. Pancho dropped the torch and the three clutched each other in fright.

'What was it?' whispered Pepita.

94

'I think it was the trap door closing,' said Antonio.

'But why would they close it?' Pancho asked trembling with fear.

'Perhaps the ghosts made them,' Pepita said and everyone shivered again.

'What shall we do now,' Pancho asked, picking up the torch.

'We'll have to go back and see what's happened,' said Antonio.

'I wish we'd never come,' wailed Pancho, and Pepita was thinking the same thing.

'Stop crying,' said Antonio trying to be brave, but looking very frightened. 'Come on, let's get going!'

He tugged on the rope and Pepita and Pancho fell into step behind him. They crept silently back along the passage, keeping close to the wall. There was no noise from anywhere now, but the air smelled even more musty than before which meant the trap door was closed and the fresh air couldn't get in.

They kept very close together as they turned the bends and when they turned the last corner into the first room they all gasped in fright and clutched each other in horror!

For there in front of them at the other end of the room were three tall figures draped in white cloth; the bodies were flat from the shoulders and on one side of each body a bent arm held something round, which looked suspiciously like a head.

THE THREE HEADLESS GHOSTS. Here they were, standing in the room which Pepita, Antonio and Pancho had passed through only a few minutes ago.

The three stood still, not daring to move. The ghosts didn't

95

move either. They stood like that for some time, the only sound in the room was the chattering of Pepita's teeth. The only movement was the flicker of the torch which hung by Pancho's side.

'We'll have to do something,' Antonio hissed at last. 'We have to get past them to get out.'

'Speak to them,' Pancho said
'They wouldn't be able to answer, would they?' Antonio said. 'Their heads are under their arms.'

'It doesn't stop them from walking about though, does it,' said Pancho.

'Do you think they're real?' Pepita breathed

'Well we can see them, can't we?'

'But perhaps they'll fade away in a few minutes. That's what ghosts usually do, isn't it?'

'Let's wait a few minutes then.'

They waited, but nothing happened. The ghosts didn't move and they didn't fade away.

'They don't seem as though they are going to harm us,' Pepita whispered at last.

'Let's go closer and see,' whispered Antonio.

'Do you think it's safe?' Pancho asked nervously.

'Let's try anyway,' Pepita whispered. 'We can't stay here all night.'

Holding hands they started to move carefully across the floor. The ghosts didn't move and the three felt a little braver as they drew nearer. As they got closer to the ghosts the torch showed them up more clearly. The white robes looked very much like sheets. Antonio reached out his hand to touch a sheet and as he did, the three sheets suddenly flew up in the air to show, there, underneath three familiar figures wearing very strange hats. At the same time three footballs dropped to the floor.

'Ha! Ha!' yelled Carlos, Hugo and Miguel, jumping down from the three boxes on which they had been standing to make them taller. 'We fooled you!'

Pepita, Antonio and Pancho were shocked and speechless. The three 'ghosts' looked at their three faces and started to laugh.

They laughed and laughed. Pepita and her brothers just looked. As they looked they got very cross. Very cross indeed.

'That was not very funny,' Pepita said at last to the laughing trio.

'So that's what you were too busy doing to come with us on the ghost hunt,' said Antonio angrily.

'You frightened us!' yelled Pancho at the top of his voice.

Carlos, Hugo and Miguel were helpless with laughter. The more angry the other three got, the more they laughed. And suddenly Antonio started to laugh and Pancho joined in. Pepita looked at her brothers and then at the three ghosts rolling on the floor in their funny hats and she began to laugh too. Finally they were all sitting on the floor laughing and laughing and nobody was cross or nervous any more.

'Where did you get those ridiculous hats,' gasped Pancho and they all burst into fresh laughter for the hats were very ridiculous. They were really planks of wood which had been padded by wrapping material around several times to make them look like shoulders. Each boy's hat was tied under the chin with ribbons. The whole idea had been to pretend their bodies started at their shoulders and the footballs were supposed to be the heads which they carried under their arms.

'If we hadn't been so frightened we would have seen through that disguise right away,' laughed Pepita and they all laughed again.

At last Antonio said: 'Well, the joke was on us, but how did you know how to get into the passages?'

'We made Maria tell us,' Carlos said. 'She didn't want to

because she knew we had said we weren't going and she didn't want to let Pepita's secret out. But in the end she agreed to go along with our joke. We told her to bang the trap door really hard after we came down.'

'Yes,' agreed Hugo, 'and when you came down, Miguel came back to the convent door to let us know you were down here and then we got into our costumes and followed you down. We crept really quietly so you wouldn't hear us.'

'We practised on Sunday so we could do it in the dark,' Miguel confessed.

'Oh, so it was you three who put up the masks to make it even more scary!' said Antonio. But the three 'ghosts' looked puzzled.

'What masks?'

'The ones on every bend, the first one is particularly horrible,' Antonio replied.

'We didn't put up any masks,' they said.

'But you must have seen the first one when you came down,' said Pepita.

'We didn't see anything because it was dark, we just felt our way here. We didn't want to shine a light in case you saw us,' said Hugo. 'But there weren't any masks on Sunday; we brought a candle and would have seen them.'

Everyone looked puzzled now. *Who* could have put the masks there? Suddenly everyone felt nervous again.

'Perhaps the *real* ghosts put them there,' Pepita said, voicing what everyone was thinking.

'Come on,' said Antonio, 'Let's get out of here, I don't think I want to meet any more ghosts tonight!'

They picked themselves off the floor feeling tired now that all the excitement was over, and shivering with cold and nervousness.

Pepita was the first to reach the steps and she led the way to the top and banged on the trap door, waiting for Maria to open up.

But nothing happened.

She banged again and everyone waited in silence.

Nothing happened.

'Bang again,' said Hugo, climbing up to help Pepita. They both banged.

Then they heard a faint voice.

'It's stuck,' Maria's voice said. 'Help us by pushing.'

Pepita and Hugo pushed but the trap door wouldn't move. The other boys all tried too, but nothing happened.

'We'll have to get help,' Maria shouted faintly and the others looked at each other in dismay.

'Maria! Wait!' Hugo shouted. But there was no reply. Maria and Leticia had left already.

The others sat on the steps. Hugo had brought a candle and some matches which he lit. With the candle and Pepita's torch there was enough light to see each other, but they were cold now. They were also afraid. It was eerie down there and who knows? Perhaps the ghosts were somewhere around?

'I wonder who they will bring?' Pepita said.

'Who knows, I hope they don't bring any grown ups or we'll really be in trouble,' said Pancho gloomily.

'I expect it will take them a while,' said Antonio, but just as he finished speaking there was a loud noise and the sound of the trap door being moved.

Suddenly it lifted out of sight and the face of Don Pedro peered down at them!

'So there you are,' he said beaming at them. 'You are brave!'

The six looked at each other in surprise. Here was an adult, Miguel's grandfather in fact, and he didn't look very cross.

'Well what are you sitting there for? Have you finished down there? Are you coming out?' Don Pedro asked.

They began to climb out into the fresh air, Pepita was first and as she climbed out she saw that the courtyard was full of light.

The light came from three lanterns. Don Pedro held one, Don Pepe held the other and Grandmother was holding the third lantern!

And not only were there three adults in the courtyard, but there, sticking her head out of the window they had climbed through, was Esperanza, her corn flowers wilting, watching the scene with great interest.

'How did Esperanza get in?' Pepita asked, so surprised to see the cow it was the first question which occurred to her.

'I have a key to the front door,' said Don Pedro, 'She followed us.' He said it as though it was quite natural for him to have a key to the front door of the convent.

By now the boys had all climbed out and were looking around with the same amazement as Pepita.

The three elderly people burst out laughing. 'Don't look so worried,' said Grandmother, 'We won't tell your parents!'

The six looked at each other, feeling very puzzled.

'Oh no,' said Don Pepe, 'We just had to come and see you because it reminded us of old times!'

Old times! The six looked at each other again.

'Yes,' said Don Pedro laughing. 'You see we used to come ghost hunting every year together.'

'Us and others,' added Grandmother and Pepita knew she meant Grandfather.

'But it took us years to find the entrance to the secret passage,' Don Pepe added.

'Really?' said Pepita, quite amazed at the three giggling grown ups who were behaving like children.

'Oh yes, that's why we think you're really clever,' said Grandmother.

'It was your grandmother who found the entrance in the end,' said Don Pedro proudly. Pepita looked at her grandmother in amazement, she couldn't imagine her being the same age as herself and going on a ghost hunt.

'It was Pepita who found the entrance for us,' Pancho said, excited by the coincidence.

'How did you find it, Grandmother?' Pepita asked, wondering if she already knew the answer.

'Well one lazy afternoon, I was sitting in that window where Esperanza is now and I was watching a pretty coloured bird fly around . . .'

'And it landed on the handle!' Pepita finished her grandmother's sentence in great excitement.

'Yes,' said Grandmother, grinning at Pepita.

'And you thought it was strange that a fountain should have a handle.' Pepita went on quickly.

'Right,' smiled Grandmother.

'What a coincidence!' shouted Antonio. 'Pepita saw a butterfly land on the handle and that's what gave her the idea.' Everyone burst out laughing.

'Did you really never see the ghosts?' asked Carlos.

'No, never,' said Don Pedro gravely. 'But we gave ourselves quite a few frights. In those days there were still things stored down there and once we found a skull!' The children looked impressed and then Antonio thought of something.

'Was it you who put the masks down there?' The three adults looked a bit uncomfortable.

'It was you wasn't it?' Antonio insisted.

'Yes,' Don Pedro said, looking a little shame-faced. 'We thought it would be more exciting for you because we knew you wouldn't find any ghosts.'

'I thought I recognised the masks,' said Antonio.

'Of course, we didn't know that Carlos, Hugo and Miguel had planned some excitement for you until we arrived and found Maria and Leticia waiting at the entrance,' said Don Pepe.

Just then, Maria and Leticia pushed Esperanza aside and climbed out of the window. They were alone, they hadn't brought anyone to help open the trap door.

'Couldn't you find anyone?' asked Antonio.

'We didn't go for anyone,' Maria said. 'It was Don Pedro's joke to make you think you were trapped. He and Don Pepe stood on the trap door while you pushed!'

Really. These grown ups, they were more childish than children.

'Oh Pepita,' said Maria, 'I'm sorry about giving your secret away to Carlos and Hugo, but they *made* me tell them,' Maria made a face at her brothers.

'That's all right,' said Pepita generously. 'But there's one thing still puzzling me.' She turned to look at her Grandmother and the two elderly men standing beside her.

'How were you so sure we would be here tonight? We didn't tell Don Pepe that we would be coming here, and how did you know that we had found the secret entrance?' Pepita stood with her hands on her hips waiting for her grandmother's answer. Grandmother looked at Pepita seriously.

'Oh Pepita, you know there is no such thing as a secret in Tepingo!' and everyone laughed. But while they laughed Pepita felt sad because she wished that sometimes it were possible to keep a secret in this village.

'Come on,' said Grandmother, 'There are no ghosts here tonight, let's go back and enjoy the feast before all the food is finished.'

Esperanza gave a loud moo of agreement and everyone set off, laughing and talking about the ghost hunt which would be remembered for many years to come.

Pepita lingered a moment to push the fountain into place again and to pick up her torch.

'So,' she thought, 'no headless ghosts after all. Still, it was quite an adventure.'

But as she climbed through the window behind the others,

something made her turn her head back to the courtyard. There was a rustling in the far corner and she saw shadows moving.

Was it the trees? Or could it be the ghosts. Pepita stood frozen, staring hard into the courtyard.

'I'm sure it's the ghosts,' she thought to herself.

But she didn't go back to find out!

TEPINGO ‧ TREASURE

It was a hot, dreamy sort of afternoon and Pepita sat with her feet in the river and her fishing line hanging from her big toe.

It was the end of the rainy season in Tepingo and the rivers were full of rushing water and quite a lot of fish. Everyone went fishing in Tepingo at the end of the rainy season, but Pepita wasn't having much luck with her lazy fishing line.

She was happy to sit in the sun, though, after all those months of damp weather. She watched the butterflies and the birds and wondered what it must be like to live in a city where people don't go fishing in rivers. Would life in the city be as beautiful as life in Tepingo, she wondered.

'Got it!' came a great yell from along the bank, so loud that Pepita almost fell into the water with shock.

'Got what?' she yelled back at her brother, Antonio, who was squirming back up the bank of the river looking very muddy.

'Look, look!' he yelled. 'I caught a fish with my hands.'

So he had. Pepita was very impressed. She had been sitting there for hours and nothing had stirred at the end of her line. Perhaps it would be better to throw the line away.

'Look, it's a really big one,' Antonio was very excited about his catch. 'Mother will be pleased.' he said, struggling up the bank to put the fish in the basket. 'Why don't you have a try, Pepita, you might have some luck.'

Pepita thought he might be right, so she turned over on her tummy and wriggled down the bank until her hands were held cupped just above the water. She could see the fish swimming under the surface and she got ready to plunge forward.

'Be careful you don't fall in,' Antonio yelled down, noticing how close she was to the water. But it was too late. Pepita suddenly pounced for a fish and the next thing Antonio heard was a big SPLASH! Pepita had fallen in.

'I told you,' Antonio yelled down, laughing at his sister who was spluttering her way to the surface. Fortunately she was a good swimmer.

'Hey, it's really nice in here,' Pepita called back. 'Let's swim down to the rapids and cool off a bit.'

Antonio dived into the water and they swam strongly down river. The rapids were not very deep ones, in fact they were rather shallow, and after the rainy season the children of Tepingo found it fun to let the water carry them quickly down stream.

The river eventually ran into a rock pool which was deep and cool and surrounded by rocks which made good diving boards.

This afternoon the pool was crowded with children from the village and Pepita and Antonio joined in the diving from the rocks. Everyone competed to see how high they could dive.

'Let's have a race down the rapids,' somebody shouted after a while, and Pepita and Antonio were among the six who agreed.

They climbed out of the pool and walked back along the river until they came to the part where the rapids began.

They lined up as best as they could across the river and Antonio called out 'Ready, steady, go.' Off they went, swimming as hard as they could in the swift water which usually carried them along without any effort. They pushed each other out of the way, jostling for the best place in the middle of the river where it was easiest to swim. Everyone got cross with everyone else for pushing, because everyone wanted to win.

Pepita had made a good start, but Antonio was in a mischievous mood. Twice he bumped into her, pushing her into the shallows and making her lose time. She caught him up and was about to bump him over to the side when he noticed her and gave her a particularly hefty shove. She slipped out of the fast flowing current onto a mud bank at the side of the river, and had difficulty getting out. She put her hands down into the mud looking for a firm surface to help her take off again.

'I'll get you for that, Antonio!' she yelled angrily to her brother, as he swam off to catch up with the others, who had overtaken them by now.

Pepita slithered around in the mud for a minute and then her hand caught on to something hard. She thought it must be a rock and gave a push to get herself back into the water, but as she pushed, the object came away in her hand and instead of moving off, she found her hand coming up, holding something, while her knees slipped further into the mud.

She looked at the heavy object in her hand. It obviously wasn't a rock, but it was so muddy she couldn't decide what it was. She made a better effort to get off the mud bank and once she had slid back into the water, started to wash the mud off this strange object.

It was the figure of a sitting man, carved out of stone.

Pepita looked at it curiously, it was a very strange figure. It didn't look like the people she knew in the village. She wondered how it could have got there. What was it?

She had forgotten about the race now, she couldn't get back to the mud flat to see if there were any more figures because the current was too strong, she let herself float along with the water, holding the figure in her hand. When she had cascaded into the pool again she looked around for Antonio. He was standing on the edge laughing at her with the other competitors who thought it was funny to see her come in last.

Pepita didn't take any notice of their laughter. She shouted to her brother.

'Come here, I've got something to show you.'

'Oh yes, I'm sure you have,' laughed Antonio, suspecting a trick.

'No, truthfully, I have, look,' she said, holding the figure above the water so he could see it. 'It's very strange, I found it up the river, come and see.'

'So long as you promise not to hit me with it,' shouted Antonio still hovering on the edge of the pool.

'Don't be stupid, come on,' Pepita shouted back and Antonio dived in and swam over to her. She considered the possibility of hitting him with the figure but thought he might drown if she did, so she decided she would be kind to him instead.

'Look,' she said and Antonio took the figure and examined it while he floated on his back.

'Don't drop it!' Pepita shouted at him and Antonio looked hurt. Pepita always suspected the worst of her brothers.

'It looks very old,' Antonio said after he had inspected it. 'Where did you find it?'

'Back there, on the mud flat which you pushed me on to.' Pepita said.

'Let's go back and take a look, maybe we'll find some more,' suggested Antonio.

They walked back along the river and scrambled down the bank to the mud flat. Their knees oozed into the mud and they made a lot of slurpy noises as they moved around, feeling for hard objects under the mud. They couldn't find anything.

'No, there aren't any more, somebody must have thrown that one away into the river and it landed in the mud,' Antonio said after a while.

But Pepita didn't think so. She had the feeling the stone carving had been lying in the mud for many years.

'I think it's very old,' Pepita said. 'I think it was made by the ancestors.'

'By the ancestors?'

'Yes, there's a book in the library that has drawings of figures like that one.'

Antonio knew his sister spent a lot of time in the library, so he was sure she was right.

'Well, let's try again,' he said, and they scrambled around in the mud for quite a long while.

111

Then, just as they were about to give up, Antonio gave a great cry.

'Pepita, I think I've found another one, it's jammed into the bank here,' she slithered down the bank to take a look and, sure enough, buried in the bank there was a smooth looking stone which looked as though it could be another figure.

They took a couple of sticks and worked it out gradually from the mud. It *was* another figure! This one looked like a woman, but it wasn't in perfect condition, part of it had rubbed away and it was difficult to tell exactly what it might have been.

Pepita was really excited now. 'Antonio, I really think we've found something very important.'

'What shall we do with the carvings?' Antonio asked.

'I'll take them to school tomorrow and ask Senorita Lopez. She might know what they are.'

Just then some of the other children came up and asked them to go to play football back in the village.

'Don't say anything to anyone,' Pepita whispered to Antonio, although she wasn't really sure why they should keep it a secret. They packed the figures in the fish basket with the fish and set off for the village. Antonio went to play football and Pepita went home to help her mother make the supper, at least they had one fish from their afternoon's expedition.

It was growing dark when Pepita arrived home and the family was gathered around a wood fire outside. Mother and Grandmother were cooking, Father was carving dolls and the little girls were playing a peaceful game. The animals had been fed and the yard was quiet and sleepy looking in the evening sunset.

112

Pepita unpacked the basket and took out the two figures. She showed them to her grandmother and her parents.

'I haven't seen anything like that before around here,' said Grandmother.

'Haven't you?' Pepita was surprised, she thought her grandmother knew about everything that was old to do with Tepingo.

'No,' Grandmother replied.

'I think they might be quite old,' Father said, examining them carefully by the firelight.

'How old?' Pepita asked.

'Oh, hundreds of years,' Father replied.

Hundreds of years. Pepita hadn't thought they would be that old.

'That means they might be quite valuable,' Mother said, as she leant over the cooking pot on the fire.

'Well sort of,' Father replied carefully. 'Really, they wouldn't be valuable in terms of money because the government doesn't allow people to sell old things that belong to the nation, but they would be valuable to the history of Tepingo, that's for sure,' he went on.

'You take the carvings to school tomorrow, Pepita, and see what your teacher says,' Grandmother told her.

Pepita couldn't sleep much that night, she was really excited about the idea that she might have discovered this important treasure. She arrived at school early, not even waiting for Maria, but there was not time to talk to Senorita Lopez when she arrived, because she started the lesson at once. Pepita had to wait until lunch time for a chance to talk to her teacher.

'Please, Senorita Lopez, I would like to show you something,' Pepita said as the teacher cleaned the blackboard.

'What is it, Pepita?' Senorita Lopez asked without turning around.

Pepita laid the carvings on her teacher's table.

'Please, Senorita, take a look at these carvings,' she said.

Senorita Lopez turned round and saw the carvings; she was obviously interested in them because she bent over and examined them for quite a long time.

'Where did you get these, Pepita?' she asked at last.

'I found them in a mud bank on the river when I was fishing with my brother yesterday,' Pepita said.

'Well, they are certainly very interesting; I have seen something similar to these in the museum in Mexico City. It would be interesting to find out whether they are real or whether they are just copies. If they are real they would have been made by the people who lived here a long time ago, but we need to know how old they are and what they are supposed to be.'

'How can we find out?' Pepita asked.

'Well, the museum would have to examine them and give them some chemical tests to find out their age, and study whether the carvings look the kind of things which are known to have come from here in the past. They would have to check the area carefully and see if there are any more statues like these.'

Pepita shook her head sadly. 'No, there aren't any more, my brother and I checked very carefully and we couldn't find any more,' she said, but the teacher smiled.

'Oh, it isn't as simple as that, Pepita.' she said. 'If there are more carvings, they are probably buried very deep under soil.

People called archaeologists would have to come and dig the area carefully, working in a special way to see whether they can find more.'

Archaeologists. Pepita tried to say the name, but it wasn't easy. Senorita Lopez laughed.

'Yes, archaeologists are people who study history by digging up the past. Old ways of living often get buried deep into the soil and these people have ways of moving the earth to find all the history underneath.'

Pepita was impressed, obviously the carvings she had found could be the beginning of something big underground near the river.

'Do you think they might find a pyramid down by the river?' Pepita asked, thinking of the pyramid in the hills which they had visited on the day of the ancestors.

'Oh, I don't think anything as big as that, Pepita, but they might find some more carved figures and perhaps some things which people used in their houses,' Senorita Lopez said.

'Why do you think the things were in the river?' Pepita asked.

'Well, at one time people used to come through Tepingo on their way to trade with other people and they probably used to make camp beside the river, so that they had plenty of water. I suppose somehow or other the carvings got left behind. It's only an idea, there could be many other explanations.'

'What shall I do with the carvings?'

Senorita Lopez could see that Pepita was very interested in the idea that she might have discovered a piece of history so she decided to help her.

'Well, I will write a letter to the Director of the Museum of

Anthropology in the city and see if we can make an appointment with him or one of his assistants to show them the carvings. If he writes back and says yes, I'll take you with me so you can hear what he says. It is the duty of anyone who finds old treasures like these to report them to the national museum.'

'Take me to the *city*. Do you really mean it?' Pepita gasped. She had never dreamed that she might go to the city, at least not until she was very grown up.

'Oh, yes I think so, it would be good for you to see the museum anyway.'

'Oh thank you, Senorita!' Pepita was almost in tears she was so excited. 'Can my brother, Antonio, come too, he found one of the carvings you know?'

'I expect he can go too, Pepita; now run along or you will miss your lunch. I'll write that letter this afternoon.'

Pepita ran outside to find Antonio and tell him the news. She could already imagine getting on the bus and riding towards the big city full of buildings and cars and streets and people in city clothes, which she had never seen and which would be very different from the sleepy village of Tepingo.

But Pepita and Antonio soon learned that things which are exciting do not happen so quickly. Senorita Lopez wrote her letter that afternoon, but weeks and weeks went by without a reply. Pepita would ask her every morning, as soon as she had arrived at school, whether she had received a reply, and every morning Senorita Lopez said the same thing.

'I'm sorry, Pepita, not today.' The teacher began to wish that she hadn't raised Pepita's hopes, because it looked as though

116

perhaps the museum wasn't very interested in two small carvings found in a river in the little village of Tepingo.

'I wish we'd never found them,' Pepita told Grandmother one day as they sat together making tortillas.

'Oh, you must be patient,' Grandmother said. 'These things don't happen in a day, Pepita.' Pepita looked at Grandmother and thought she would die with impatience, but her Grandmother twinkled back at her and Pepita thought perhaps she could live another day.

It was just as well that Pepita decided not to die of impatience, because when she walked into the classroom next morning, Senorita Lopez spoke to her before she could ask the usual question.

'It's come, Pepita, here it is,' she said, waving an envelope in Pepita's direction, and Pepita burst into a smile. But Senorita Lopez looked very serious and Pepita wondered if perhaps the news wasn't good from the museum.

'Sit down, Pepita. I'll read the letter aloud so everyone can hear it,' she said.

Pepita wasn't too happy about that, she didn't feel like sharing bad news with about thirty other people, but there was no arguing with Senorita Lopez, so she sat down and waited for the worst.

'Well everyone,' Senorita Lopez told the class, 'you know that a few weeks ago (was it only a few weeks, Pepita thought, it seemed like years) Pepita and her brother, Antonio, found two stone carvings in the river here in Tepingo. They are very unusual, and it seems that they might have been carved by the ancestors. I wrote to the museum to see whether they would be interested in having a look at the carvings and this is the reply I have received today.'

Everyone watched with interest as she took the letter out of the envelope, put on her glasses and began to read.

'Dear Senorita Lopez, We are most interested to hear of the find of two stone carvings in the village of Tepingo. (Pepita's heart leapt in excitement) We are pleased that you carried out your duty in reporting this archaeological find to us.'

Here, Senorita Lopez looked over the letter at Pepita. Pepita felt very important, she was the only person in the class who knew what the word archaeological meant, and so she was the only one who knew how important the find could be.

'The director of the museum would like you to bring the carvings to the museum for examination by a specialist in your area of the country. The museum will be happy to pay your expenses to make the visit, and will also pay for the two children who made the find, so that they can visit the museum.'

Everyone burst out clapping when Senorita Lopez read this part of the letter, and Pepita wriggled with excitement. The teacher carried on reading.

We enclose a cheque to cover the bus fares to the city and we hope to hear from you soon as to which date is most convenient for you to visit the museum.'

Everybody started talking at once. The children were jealous

118

of Pepita, but they were also pleased that somebody in their class had made such an important find and had been invited to the city to show it to people who were such experts. Senorita Lopez told Pepita they could go to the museum next week and that she would write that day to make the appointment.

'We'll have to tell the mayor, of course,' said Senorita Lopez. 'After all the carvings belong to Tepingo and he should know what is going on here. I'll go along and see him after school and we'll get on the bus to the city on Monday. Now, let's get on with some work.'

It was difficult for Pepita to concentrate on her work that day, and she was glad when she was finally walking home with Maria.

'It's really exciting, Pepita,' Maria said.

'Yes, I never believed that I would go to the city until I grew up, and especially not to take treasure with me! I wish you could come too, Maria.'

'So do I,' said Maria a little sadly. 'Just think of all the things you will see, cars and houses and offices and shops and restaurants.'

'Yes,' said Pepita, 'and the museum. I've heard it's very beautiful, and full of history from all over the country.'

'Yes, there are some pictures of it in the library,' Maria said. 'There is a beautiful fountain in the courtyard and all the floors are made of marble.'

'Senorita Lopez said we would have to eat our lunch in a restaurant.' Pepita said, looking at Maria with wide eyes.

'You mean sit at a table and eat with a knife and a fork?' Maria asked.

'Yes,' Pepita said, looking a bit frightened.

'Oh well, Senorita Lopez will tell you what to do.'

'Yes, I expect she will,' Pepita said, looking gratefully at her friend.

Everyone wanted to hear all about the letter when Pepita and Antonio got home. They had heard the news before the children arrived. News travels fast in Tepingo, so fast that nobody really knows how it gets there.

'Well, didn't I tell you that you had to be patient?' demanded Grandmother and Felipe the parrot squawked with laughter when he heard Grandmother talk like that.

'We'll have to get your school uniforms mended, and you'll have to have a good wash in the river on Sunday, if you're going to the city,' Mother said sternly, but Pepita could tell she was pleased and Father was already telling Antonio the tale of how he once went to the big city.

Time passed slowly in the next few days and on Sunday Pepita and Antonio followed Mother's instructions and had a good scrub in the river. Pepita woke early on Monday and found that Grandmother was already up and about.

'Come, I'll braid your hair carefully for you,' Grandmother said, 'I've bought you a new piece of pink ribbon.'

Pepita hugged the old lady. Grandmother always knew how to make special days even more special.

She sat down on the floor in front of the fire while Grandmother brushed her hair.

'Now, Pepita, you won't get lost will you?' Grandmother asked anxiously.

'I hope not, Grandmother,' Pepita replied.

'Well you know what you're like, you're always thinking up big adventures, but let me tell you it would not be very exciting to get lost in such a big city. It will be very frightening and I think you had better stay close to Senorita Lopez and keep an eye on Antonio.'

Pepita patted her grandmother's hand, she could feel how worried she was about her grandchildren going off to the big city.

The bus was leaving at seven o'clock for the city and Antonio and Pepita had arranged to meet Senorita Lopez at the bus stop in the village square at a quarter to seven. Father had left for the fields long ago and Mother was busy organising breakfast and getting the other children ready. So when it was time to leave, Pepita and Antonio waved goodbye to their family from the gates. Grandmother gave them some money to spend on sweets in the city and Mother gave them a little package of food to eat on the bus. Pepita carried the carvings in a basket. Father had wrapped them and packed them very carefully so that they wouldn't get broken on the way.

'Take good care,' Grandmother called anxiously.

'We will,' they called back as they set off down the road.

'Remember everything so that you can tell us when you come back,' Mother called out.

'We'll write it all down on our way back,' Pepita shouted, knowing she had brought a notebook and some paper to do just that. Somehow she had a funny feeling Senorita Lopez would want her to write about her day too!

As they walked along the street they saw Esperanza the cow leaning over the wall of her field looking a little sad.

121

'Good morning, Esperanza,' said Pepita. 'I'm sorry you can't come with us, but I'll tell you all about it when I get back.'

'Moo,' said Esperanza sadly. Cows never got much of a chance of an outing.

Pepita and Antonio arrived at the square a little early and they sat down to wait for Senorita Lopez who was usually very

punctual. But they were getting worried by ten to seven when Senorita Lopez hadn't turned up.

'Where could she be?' Pepita said, bobbing up and down looking for her teacher.

122

'I don't know,' Antonio said. 'She's usually always on time.'

They looked at each other anxiously. Was it possible that she wouldn't turn up? It would be awful if she didn't come.

The bus pulled up at the side of the road and people started to climb aboard. Pepita and Antonio felt desperate. Senorita Lopez had the tickets so they couldn't get on and take their seats. Just then, they saw Anita Perez rushing up towards them. Anita lived with Senorita Lopez and did her housework for her.

'Pepita, Antonio, wait,' she called as though they were about to leave on the bus. 'I'm sorry, I've got bad news to tell you.' Pepita and Antonio looked at each other in dismay.

'Senorita Lopez is ill, very ill, she's very sorry but she can't come. She said she will take you another day. Here are the tickets. You are to ask the driver for the money back so that you can go another time. I have to run back. She's very ill.' And with that, Anita Perez ran back along the road.

Pepita and Antonio felt numb with shock. They watched Anita running away and Pepita held the tickets in hands which were beginning to tremble. Tears came into her eyes.

'Pepita, I can't believe it,' Antonio said, choking back his own tears.

Pepita looked at her brother's unhappy face and made a very quick decision. Why should they be so unhappy?

'Quick, Antonio, get on the bus!' she shouted and started to pull him towards the bus.

'What do you mean get on the bus, Pepita, we can't go alone.'

'Yes we can,' said Pepita. 'Come on, quickly, it's going.'

Without knowing what he was doing Antonio allowed Pepita

123

to drag him through the knot of people who were saying goodbye to relatives around the bus and up the stairs.

The driver was so busy taking tickets and organising everyone he didn't notice two children climbing aboard by themselves, so they moved quickly down to the back of the bus, hoping he wouldn't notice them and settled into their seats. The bus started up straight away and they didn't have time to change their minds.

'Keep your head down, Antonio,' Pepita hissed, 'we don't want people to spot us in here on our own.'

The two ducked down beneath the window as the bus drove out of Tepingo and it was just as well they did, because Grandmother and the little girls were waiting at the corner of the road to the house, to wave goodbye as the bus went past.

'They must be sitting on the other side and they didn't see us,' Grandmother said to the little girls as the bus sped by.

'Phew!' said Pepita a few minutes later. 'We did it, Antonio. We're on our way to the city.'

'Mother and Father will be furious when we get back,' Antonio said, looking very gloomy.

'Oh, let's worry about that when we get back,' Pepita said determined to enjoy the day now that she had made her decision. 'I didn't wait all those weeks just to find out I couldn't go.'

'But how will we find our way to the museum?' Antonio asked.

'We'll ask,' Pepita said. 'We've got the money which Grandmother gave us, we'll just have to ask which bus to get on. Now stop worrying and enjoy the ride.'

Already the bus was some miles from the village in open

124

country and soon the road started to twist upward towards the city which was over a mile high. Grandmother had made them bring sweaters because she thought it must be very chilly in the city because it was so high up.

It took the bus more than two hours to get to the outside of the city and Pepita watched the road every second of the way.

Suddenly there were more and more cars surrounding the bus as it made its way to the city. In the distance she could see buildings and smoke coming from factories and then the bus started to go down a hill and there, spread before them, was the whole city. It was full of houses and office buildings, factories and long streets.

Pepita and Antonio had never seen anything like it in their whole lives. In Tepingo when they looked into the distance they saw hills and fields, rivers and flowers. Here, all they could see were buildings and cars, and now the buildings were all around them and it was only possible to see a few yards ahead. More buildings blocked the view, and when they looked up the buildings were very tall and it wasn't possible to see much of the sky. When they did see the sky, it wasn't blue, as it was in Tepingo, it was a sort of dirty grey and Pepita thought it was probably the smoke from the factories and the cars.

Outside the windows of the bus many people hurried along the streets, looking as though they had important appointments to keep, nobody ever walked very fast in Tepingo, and here there were so many people walking fast.

Apart from the buildings, the cars and the people there was something else which amazed Pepita. The *noise*. She hadn't thought the city could be so noisy. She could hardly hear a word Antonio was saying as he kept pointing to things outside the bus. Tepingo was noisy, too, but in a different way; there it was animals and babies and music from the fiestas, it was a more peaceful noise somehow.

'What a noisy place,' she said loudly to Antonio.

'Yes, and dirty and big,' Antonio said, looking rather nervous.

Pepita clutched the carvings closely to her, feeling a bit nervous herself. It had been her decision to come here and she would have to get them out of the mess now. She clutched the two carvings even tighter; she had heard stories of people stealing things in cities.

The bus seemed as though it were never going to stop. It drove through streams of traffic now, honking at crazy drivers and the passengers were jolted all over the place. Pepita and Antonio laughed every time the bus stopped at a traffic light.

'Fancy a big bus like this stopping because of a little red light,' they said. They had never seen traffic lights before.

'Look, Antonio,' Pepita clutched her brother's arm. 'That must be a restaurant.' She pointed to a collection of tables which were outside a shop window. People were sitting at the tables and eating. They looked very smartly dressed. Pepita looked down with dismay at the school uniform which her mother had so carefully mended and pressed.

'Oh Pepita, look at all those cinemas.' They were passing down a street full of cinemas with big advertisements outside. In Tepingo there was a film once a month in the village hall. Antonio never missed a film, he loved seeing them.

Eventually the bus roared into a huge bus station, very different from the roadside stop in Tepingo. This place was full of large buses from all over the country and hundreds of people were getting on and off.

'How are we going to find out how we get to the museum,' Antonio asked again, looking very worried.

'Stop worrying!' Pepita snapped, showing just how nervous she was herself.

As she got off the bus, Pepita looked up at the driver who was helping the passengers get down. 'Could you tell us please how to get to the Museum of Anthropology?' she asked.

The bus driver looked at Pepita and Antonio very suspiciously.

'Did you travel here by yourselves?' he demanded.

'Oh yes, here are our tickets,' she handed them over to the driver. 'We are going to meet our aunt at the museum.'

'Why didn't she come here to meet you?' the bus driver wanted to know.

'She's not very well and it's too far for her to come,' Pepita smiled at the driver. Antonio was digging her in the ribs, frightened that she was telling lies. But the bus driver didn't have time to waste on a couple of children.

'Go up the stairs and look for the desk marked INFORMA-TION, they'll tell you how to get to the museum.'

Pepita and Antonio headed straight for the stairs.

'How could you tell lies like that?' Antonio asked as they hurried along.

Pepita felt rather guilty about finding it so easy to tell lies, but if she hadn't they wouldn't have been able to get away so easily. She raced ahead of her brother holding on hard to the basket with the statues.

At the top of the stairs there was the sign saying INFORMA-TION. Pepita didn't hesitate, she went straight up to the desk. The woman behind the desk didn't seem surprised that two children were asking the way to the museum.

'You go out of the main door, turn right and find the 29 bus, it stops right in front of the museum,' she said.

Pepita and Antonio walked towards the main door. There were people everywhere and they had to push their way through the crowd.

'Be careful with the basket,' Antonio hissed and Pepita clutched it very tightly with both hands.

Outside on the pavement there were more people and they all looked as though they knew where they were going. Pepita and Antonio had never been among so many people in such a hurry before and there were so many buses lined up across the street it was hard to tell which was theirs. But they were too frightened to ask anyone, so they walked along the street peering at the numbers.

'Here it is,' Antonio said at last and they ran towards a bus which was about to leave, very full of passengers.

'Quick,' Pepita shouted, 'we must get on that one or we're going to be late.'

They pushed their way up the steps behind the people and had just managed to hold on to the rail, when the bus started off with a jolt which threw the passengers off balance.

'Hey, you two down there,' the bus driver shouted at Pepita and Antonio. 'Pass your fares up, don't think I didn't see you sneaking on to the bus at the last moment.'

Pepita and Antonio were dismayed that the driver thought they were trying to get a free lift on his bus, but they were too scared to explain.

'How much is the fare?' Pepita managed to ask. 'We want to go to the museum.'

'Thirty cents each,' growled the bus driver.

It was a struggle to get the money out of their pockets without falling off the steps where they stood. Then, just as they had found the money and passed the fare up to the driver, the bus stopped with another jolt and a crowd of people began pushing Pepita and Antonio up the steps and into the bus. Life in the city wasn't easy, Pepita and Antonio were learning.

Other people had got off the bus at the other end so there was room for them to stand, but they had to hold on to each other for support because they couldn't reach the straps above their heads.

They felt very miserable and began to wish they had waited until Senorita Lopez had got better.

'Where are you going, you two?' They looked up into the kindly face of an older woman.

'We want to go to the museum,' Antonio explained, 'but we can't see out of the windows to tell when we arrive.'

The woman smiled. 'Yes, it's not easy to travel in city buses is it? Where are you from?'

Pepita and Antonio were alarmed that the woman realised they didn't live in the city. But when they looked round at the other people on the bus they realised their clothes were different from city people's.

'We're from Tepingo,' Pepita said.

'From Tepingo, and you've come to see the museum?

'Yes,' said Pepita.

'Well, I'll tell you when to get off the bus. You can hold on to my basket until we get there so you don't fall over.'

It took a long time for the bus to travel through the city, for every few yards it stopped to let passengers on or off. Finally the woman prodded them.

'Now, the museum is the next stop, but you'll have to cross the road to get there, be very careful as you cross. Start moving down the bus now.'

Pepita and Antonio thanked the woman and struggled through the passengers to the end of the bus.

She was right about the road. There were six lanes of traffic, three going one way, three going the other and they were all full.

'We'll never get across,' Antonio said.

'Perhaps if we walk to the corner it will be easier,' Pepita said, but it still took them ten minutes to cross the road safely.

Once they were across they found themselves outside a large modern building, looking up into the face of a giant stone carving of a strange figure. The figure had been placed in front of the building.

Pepita read the sign at the bottom of the statue. 'Tlaloc – God of Rain' it said.

'This must have been one of the Gods which the ancestors used to worship,' she said to Antonio.

131

A man who was also standing looking at the statue heard Pepita and he said: 'Yes, the ancestors believed there was a god who made the rain. When there was no rain for the crops in the fields they would pray to this Tlaloc to make it rain. Of course, we don't believe in the old gods now, but it's a funny thing, when they brought this statue here to the museum it rained for four days and four nights without stopping and the whole city was flooded!'

Pepita and Antonio looked at the man with surprise and then they looked up at the huge stone carving. Was it possible that this stone figure had some kind of magic power over the rain? But there was no time to waste, they were already late for their appointment and the man showed them the way to the entrance.

The museum was a modern building and very big. Pepita and Antonio felt very small looking up at the large concrete and glass building. When they found the courage to push open a glass door and go inside they saw that the entrance hall led out into a courtyard into which water poured.

'Look at that, Pepita,' breathed Antonio.

'Yes,' gasped Pepita, amazed at the beauty of the fountain.

They stood and stared at the running water for many minutes before they remembered they had an appointment to keep.

'Who can we ask where we go?' Pepita said looking round.

'What was the name of the man we should see?' Antonio asked.

'Senor Ortiz,' Pepita replied.

'Let's ask the man selling tickets,' Antonio said.

They walked timidly over the shiny marble floor towards the ticket desk.

'Please, we have an appointment with Senor Ortiz,' Pepita said, looking up into the man's face.

'An *appointment*?' the man's voice boomed through the hall. Pepita and Antonio were too frightened to answer him.

'Do you have a letter about this appointment?' he asked.

The letter. Antonio and Pepita looked at each other in alarm. Pepita gulped.

Antonio looked at the floor.

The man looked at them both.

'We . . . we forgot it,' Pepita stammered at last.

'Oh yes, a likely story!' the man said looking as though he didn't believe a word.

Pepita was close to tears now and she didn't know what to say. Antonio was wishing they had never come.

Just then the man picked up a telephone on his desk and dialled a number. Pepita and Antonio had never used a telephone before and they were interested to see how it worked, but they were also frightened the man was going to call the police.

'Senorita Curiel, this is reception. I have two children down here who say they have an appointment with Senor Ortiz. Is that true?'

The man listened to the voice at the other end, then he said, 'Yes, that's right by themselves . . . er, just a minute.'

The man looked at Antonio and Pepita.

'Where are you from?' he snapped.

'Tepingo,' Antonio said.

The man repeated this to the woman on the telephone who said something. The man put the phone down looking very cross.

'She says you're to go up,' he said.

134

Pepita and Antonio grinned at each other.

'Through that door marked OFFICE and up the stairs – the next time remember the letter.'

Pepita and Antonio skipped for joy as they went towards the door.

'What a disagreeable man,' Antonio said.

'People in the city do seem to be rude,' Pepita agreed.

The woman who was waiting for them at the top of the stairs didn't look very pleased either.

'Where is Senorita Lopez?' she demanded.

'She's ill,' Pepita said.

The woman looked at her suspiciously.

'Well, you'd better come in, Senor Ortiz is waiting. You are late.'

Pepita and Antonio felt very nervous when they were shown into the large, beautifully furnished office which had a carpet. They had never walked on a carpet before and they wondered if they should take off their shoes.

But the man behind the desk didn't look cross like the other people they had met in the museum. He smiled, stood up and walked across to them, holding out his hand for them to shake.

'Well, here you are at last,' he said in a friendly tone. 'I hope you didn't get lost. I'm sorry to hear your teacher is not well, you were very brave to come on your own.'

Pepita and Antonio were beginning to feel better.

'Now come and sit down and show me what you have brought.' Senor Ortiz led them over to some chairs and they all sat down.

'Tell me again the story of how you found the statues,' he

135

said, and as Pepita unpacked her basket, Antonio told Senor Ortiz about the day they were fishing.

'Here they are,' said Pepita as Antonio finished his story. Senor Ortiz picked up the statues and examined them very carefully. He got up and went over to his desk and took out a large magnifying glass which he used to check the statues.

Pepita and Antonio watched him in suspense, hardly daring to breathe. Supposing they were fakes? Would he be very angry with them? Finally Senor Ortiz looked up.

'They are certainly very interesting, but I want to do some more tests, I'll tell you what I'll do. I'll have somebody show you round the museum and give you lunch in the restaurant and after lunch you can come back and see me and I'll tell you what I think. Is that all right with you?'

Pepita and Antonio could hardly believe their ears! They stared with wide eyes at Senor Ortiz. Was it really possible he was giving them such a treat?

Senor Ortiz laughed and rang a buzzer on his desk. A young man came in through the door behind his desk.

'Ah Carlos, here are Antonio and Pepita, you remember they are the ones who found the statues in Tepingo. I want you to show them round the museum, they have never seen it before. Then give them lunch in the restaurant. Bring them back here after lunch.'

Carlos smiled in a kindly way at the two children who were obviously from a village.

'Is this your first time in a city?'

'Yes, Senor,' said Antonio.

'Well the museum is the best thing here. Come on and we'll do a grand tour.'

He was right, it was a grand tour. Carlos really knew the history of Mexico, and he made his tour very interesting with lots of stories from different regions of the country. He led Pepita and

Antonio through room after room of statues and models. There were copies of pyramids and parts of the carvings found on them, there was a great stone calendar, carved by the Aztecs and

completely accurate and there were precious jewels and even books made out of the bark of trees.

In fact there were so many fascinating things to see that Antonio and Pepita didn't feel at all tired or hungry until Carlos said, 'It's two o'clock, we'd better find some lunch.'

Now they did feel scared! The restaurant was very elegant with white tablecloths and lots of cutlery and glasses and people looking very smart sitting round them.

'What would you like to eat?' Carlos asked as a waiter brought a menu to their table.

Pepita and Antonio didn't know what to ask for. At home their mother just gave them their food, usually a bowl of beans with tortillas and sometimes some meat and sauces.

Carlos saw the concerned look on their faces. 'Don't worry, I'll order for you,' he said cheerfully,

He ordered soup, then plates of rice with banana, then meat and vegetables and a dish of beans and then ice cream.

'Do you think that's enough?' he asked them.

Pepita and Antonio stared at him. That sounded like enough to eat for a week. Carlos laughed again.

'Now tell me what you think of the museum,' he said.

'Oh we think it's wonderful,' Pepita said. 'I think we should have one in Tepingo.'

'What, as big as this,' Carlos laughed.

'No, a smaller one, but with good things from our area,' Pepita had obviously been thinking about this.

'We haven't got anywhere we could put a museum,' Antonio said.

'Yes we have,' said Pepita

'Where?' asked Antonio.

'In the old convent, nobody ever uses it for anything.'

Carlos was interested. 'Yes, I've seen the old convent in Tepingo. You're right, it would make a good place to put a museum. Perhaps something could be done.'

'Do you think so?' Pepita sounded really pleased.

'Oh, I don't know, don't get too excited about the idea, a lot of people would have to be asked a lot of questions and make a lot of decisions. You know how these things go don't you?'

'Well, no, not really,' Pepita replied. 'In Tepingo we just ask the mayor.'

Carlos laughed and just then the waiter brought the food.

The soup came in large bowls and Pepita and Antonio watched Carlos as he put a napkin on his lap and picked up a spoon. When he started to eat, they started to eat too, they had used spoons before but something was missing. They looked at each other and Carlos saw their look.

'Waiter,' he called, 'Bring us some tortillas please.'

Pepita and Antonio looked relieved, so they had tortillas in the city too, and they felt better when they had one in their hands.

'I love tortillas,' said Carlos.

'So do we,' said Antonio.

'Yes, our grandmother makes the best tortillas in the world,' Pepita grinned happily.

'Then I'd like to meet your grandmother,' Carlos said. 'Perhaps you will invite me to visit you in Tepingo.'

Pepita and Antonio looked surprised.

139

'Really, I'd like to, now tell me more about Tepingo.'

So they spent the rest of the meal telling Carlos about Tepingo. They told him about their family and friends and Esperanza and the river and the convent and the day they went to the pyramid in the hills and much more. When the other courses came, they watched how Carlos used his knife and fork and they used theirs in the same way. It felt very strange to eat like that, but they were so busy talking they soon got used to it.

When they had finished their ice cream, Carlos said, 'Come on, we'd better go and see Senor Ortiz again or you'll miss your bus home.'

They began to feel nervous again. What would Senor Ortiz say? And how would they find their way back to the bus station?

Senor Ortiz was waiting for them in his office. The two statues were on his desk.

'I've tested them very carefully,' he said when they were all sitting down again. 'I think they are genuine and about five hundred years old. They date to about the time the Spanish came and conquered our country.' He got up and walked towards Pepita and Antonio, holding out his hand again.

'I would like to congratulate you on making a very important find.' They shook hands solemnly with Senor Ortiz and Carlos gave them a big grin. They felt rather embarrassed with such a ceremony.

'Well, we will have to keep the statues here and enter them in our records.' Pepita looked a bit upset about this.

'But they belong to Tepingo' she said.

'Well, really, anything like this, which is the treasure of the ancestors, belongs to the whole country, Pepita,' Senor Ortiz explained very kindly. 'That's why we have a national museum so that everyone can come and see the nation's treasure and learn its history.'

'But some places have their own museum,' Pepita said. 'The people of Tepingo can't afford to come to the city very often.'

'That's true,' Senor Ortiz said, 'but Tepingo doesn't have a museum, does it?'

Then Carlos spoke. 'Well as a matter of fact, Senor Ortiz, Pepita has a very good idea,' he said, and Senor Ortiz looked at him.

'She thinks Tepingo could use the convent there as a local museum and you know, it's not a bad idea,' he went on. 'The convent belongs to the nation too, it's an old monument which was given to the government many years ago. As far as I know it has never been used for anything since that time.'

'It hasn't,' said Pepita

'Except for ghost hunts,' giggled Antonio, but nobody took any notice of him.

'I expect that's because there's never been any money to look after it,' Carlos said. 'But if it became a museum, the national museum would give some money, and maybe the local people could use some of the rooms for their own activities too.' Carlos had obviously been thinking very seriously about what Pepita had to say. She looked at him gratefully.

'I'm sure if you talk to the mayor he would say yes,' Pepita said eagerly.

'You have a lot of faith in your mayor,' Senor Ortiz laughed.

'Well, it's worth a thought, but we can't give you a definite answer yet. We'd have to send a team of archaeologists to see what else they can find before we could give you some of the Tepingo collection from here. But I'll have to talk to your mayor and see what he says.' Senor Ortiz smiled at Pepita.

'Oh thank you,' Pepita said.

'And talking of your mayor, I'm going to give him a ring. I know he has a telephone and he can send a message to your parents, they will be very worried about you, you know.'

'Oh no!' Pepita and Antonio cried out at the same time.

'Oh yes,' Senor Ortiz was very firm. 'I really think that would be best.'

'How did you know our families didn't know?' Antonio asked.

'I could tell by your faces,' Senor Ortiz said. 'Now, Carlos will drive you in his car back to the bus station and make sure you get on the right bus.'

So there was nothing to be done. By the time they got back to Tepingo, everyone would know what they had done. Somehow the day didn't seem so bright any more. They shook hands politely with Senor Ortiz and went out with Carlos to his car.

'Cheer up,' said Carlos, 'I'm sure everything will be all right, everyone will be proud of you and perhaps you'll get your museum.'

He cheered them up on the way to the bus station by giving them a tour of the city, they drove down the elegant Reforma Avenue and saw the golden Angel on top of her tall column which had once fallen down in an earthquake. Then they saw the shops along the Alameida Avenue and the park where people were strolling in the late afternoon. Finally he drove them around the great square called the Zocalo, where the President lived in a fine palace.

It had certainly been quite a day for Antonio and Pepita, this day in the city, and they felt very tired as they said goodbye to Carlos and climbed aboard the bus.

Antonio fell asleep but Pepita took out her notebook and spent the journey writing down all the adventures of their day, so that she could tell everyone at home – if they weren't too cross to listen to her.

It was night by the time the bus started driving down the valley into the village and Pepita looked out of the window at the few lights in the village and thought it looked a very small place after the city.

'Wake up, Antonio.' She prodded her brother. 'We're here. We're in Tepingo.'

Antonio groaned. He didn't want to wake up and face the family, he would have preferred to stay asleep.

When the bus swung into the street which led to the village square they got up and started moving towards the front; there weren't many passengers on board for the return journey.

They looked out of the big window at the front of the bus and were very surprised at what they saw.

'Look, Pepita,' Antonio grabbed his sister's arm. 'Look at all those people out there in the square.'

'What are they doing?' Pepita was alarmed. It would be difficult to slip off the bus and make their way quietly home now.

The square was absolutely full of people and light and as the bus roared to a stop in the square, a big cheer went up from all the people. They had been waiting for the bus.

'What is happening? Who are they waiting for?' Pepita asked looking around the bus at the very few sleepy passengers who were getting their things ready to get off.

'I don't know, Pepita,' Antonio said heading back to the other end of the bus, 'but I think we'll let everyone else get off first so we can sneak off last.'

Pepita followed him back down the bus and they waited in their seats, not daring to look out of the window, until all the passengers had got off.

'Well they don't seem to be cheering anybody now,' Pepita said glumly.

'Come on, you two,' the bus driver called to them, 'there's somebody waiting for you.'

'Oh dear, it must be Father,' said Antonio. 'Come on, we'd better go and get it over with.'

They started for the front of the bus and as they got up and walked down the aisle, they noticed that the crowd suddenly pressed closer to the windows to take a look at Pepita and Antonio. And everybody was cheering.

Pepita and Antonio looked at each other in alarm. What was going on?

Pepita was first to the top of the steps and as she looked down she saw beneath her the face of the mayor, who was beaming a big smile up at her!

'Well done, Pepita,' he said. 'We welcome you for what you have done for Tepingo today. Come down and let me be the first to congratulate you.'

Welcome her? Congratulate her? Pepita couldn't understand what was going on at all, but the mayor held out his hand and she went down to shake it. Antonio followed and they were both swamped by people shaking their hands and embracing them and congratulating them and this went on for such a long time, Pepita thought she was going to faint and she felt very confused.

Finally the mayor pushed his way through the crowd and held up his hand for silence. Everyone fell quiet and stood around ready to listen to him

'As you all know,' he began, 'a few weeks ago Pepita and Antonio found some carved figures in the river here and today they took them to the museum and found out that they are very old.

'This afternoon I received a phone call from the Assistant Director of the Museum, Senor Ortiz, who told me that the carvings could be the beginning of a very important find here in Tepingo.'

Here the mayor paused to look at Pepita and Antonio who were still wriggling with embarrassment.

'He told me he will be sending a team of archaeologists here very soon and he is sure they will find many more interesting things which are important to our history here in Tepingo.

'He also told me that since Pepita and Antonio had left his office he had spoken to the Director of the Museum about Pepita's idea for a museum of our own here in Tepingo.'

The mayor paused again and looked at Pepita, he looked very solemn, and she thought he might be angry because she had suggested the idea without talking to him first.

But then the mayor's face broke into a smile and he said,

'The Director tells me he is willing to give us some money to help us start our own museum in the convent and that he is sending a Senor Carlos Mendez to Tepingo very soon to help us start work on the building, so that it will be ready for the Tepingo Collection of History.'

Everyone burst out clapping, stamping their feet and jumping around for joy. It wasn't very often that Tepingo received any attention from the outside world and to have a museum was most important. If a village had a museum, people came from all over the country to see it and Tepingo wouldn't just be a little dot on a map which nobody visited any more.

Pepita and Antonio were so surprised that all this had happened so quickly after they had left the museum they could hardly believe what was going on. They were very proud, of course, but they were also a little surprised that nobody had told them off yet for going to the city alone.

Then as the mayor was shaking their hands again, Father appeared. He stood in front of them and looked down at them very sternly.

'Well, you two have certainly had an adventure, haven't you?' he said, sounding very cross and Pepita and Antonio looked down at the floor.

'The Director of the Museum has asked me not to punish you this time because of what you have done for Tepingo.' Pepita and Antonio looked up at him more hopefully, 'But I think you should go home right now and apologise to your mother and do not leave the house again until I give you permission.'

Pepita and Antonio slipped away from the crowd and walked

silently home. They were proud of what they had done but now they were sorry they had upset their family.

'Never mind, Pepita,' Antonio squeezed her hand. 'They'll forgive us in time and just think, Carlos will be here soon and it will be fun showing him around Tepingo.'

Pepita brightened up a bit and just then Esperanza stuck her head over the wall.

'Moo,' she said looking very pleased to see that they were back.

'Oh Esperanza, it is good to see you,' Pepita said putting her arms around the cow's neck and giving her a hug. 'It seems a very long time since I last saw you, the city is not at all like Tepingo, you know.'

Esperanza nuzzled up against Pepita's arms and, as Antonio walked on to the house by himself, Pepita looked up at the tall hills which surrounded Tepingo and at the clear sky full of stars above the hills and she listened to the familiar noises of the village around her and she said: 'It was lovely to see the city, but now I know that I love Tepingo best of any place in the world.'

Esperanza gave a moo of agreement, she could have told Pepita that this morning, if she had bothered to stop to listen.